COPY

SUSAN RUSHES IN

by

JANE SHAW

THE CHILDREN'S PRESS
LONDON AND GLASGOW

FOR

JOAN LUCY WILMOTH
who used to live in Tollgate Road

PRINTED IN GREAT BRITAIN

CONTENTS

CHAPTER ONE

A JOB FOR SUSAN

IT WAS late when the girls came home from school
for the summer holidays; late and dark because they
had been held up by a railway strike at Paddington.
They had enjoyed the strike very much, only
towards evening it became a bit boring because
they were all nearly mad with hunger. Bill, who
was only eleven and didn't yet go to boarding-school
but to the local prep school, was in bed but not
asleep. Charlotte, Midge and Susan sat on his bed
and told him about the strike and caught up with
the local news—the most exciting item of which
was, of course, that they were going to Switzerland
for holidays in two weeks' time and everybody
agreed that they didn't know how they were going
to exist till then. Then Chang, Susan's Siamese cat,
had lost himself for two days and had been discovered in an immensely tall elm in the park behind
the house. "The silly ass had climbed up," said
Bill, "and was too frightened to come down. We
had to get the fire-brigade!" The girls were very
sorry to have missed that, only Susan wondered
what on earth had made Chang take to tree-
climbing in his old age and Bill said darkly the
boy next door, probably. But before anyone could
comment on that, Aunt Lucy came in to chase the
girls off to supper and bed.

"Oh, and Susan," said Bill—anything to keep

them there talking—"there's a job waiting for you —poor old Mrs. Thorne is going to be put out of her little house by that artist Pilkington, you know the chap who goes about with corduroy trousers and paint on his pullover—" but Aunt Lucy firmly pushed the girls out of Bill's room and put his light out.

Susan was Susan Lyle, she was a Scot, but she went to school with her cousins and lived with them and Uncle Charles and Aunt Lucy in Wichwood Village, a suburb of London, in the holidays, because her father had gone to build a bridge in South Africa and her mother had gone with him. Uncle Charles was a doctor; he was the father of Charlotte and Midge and Bill; but Aunt Lucy was their Aunt Lucy too who looked after them, for their mother had died when Bill was quite small.

As soon as Midge and Susan had had breakfast next morning they started on their usual ritual visit to all their special little pet places—they inspected the garden, inspected Bill's goldfish in the round basin of the disused fountain, round which grew Solomon's-seal and lily-of-the-valley in springtime. Then they walked through the kitchen garden to the little orchard, had a look to see how the apples were coming on, tried a Ribston pippin, which wasn't a success, and leant up against the weeping willow tree for a minute, watching a young frog hopping round the fringe of the pond which lay in that corner of the garden, and into which Chang, Susan *and* Aunt Lucy had fallen on one famous occasion.*

* See *Susan Pulls the Strings.*

The house next door had been empty so long that the Carmichaels had grown into the habit of using the garden as if it belonged to them. It was the scene of many of Bill's explorations and wild games, with what Midge called his horrid little prep school pals; for years the Carmichaels had feasted off the fruit from the trees and Aunt Lucy had made jam from the gooseberries. At this minute Midge and Susan were pushing their way through the tumble-down gate between the gardens and making a bee-line for a peach-tree that was trained against a south wall hiding the house, and which, Midge assured Susan, had the most wonderful peaches that anyone could imagine, she only hoped that there were a couple of ripe ones left.

"Someone has been tidying up this garden," Midge observed, glancing casually round.

"Mm. Keeping ducks too," said Susan, nodding towards a couple of Khaki Campbells who were rooting about under the hedge.

Midge stopped to look at the ducks. "I wonder if that's why our pond is so free of duck-weed," she said. "I noticed it at the time and thought that perhaps Bill had been clearing it although I must say it seemed most unlikely. I wonder if these ducks go through the hedge to our pond? I call that cheek. I thought we were the only people allowed to use this garden."

"Somebody else must have got permission," said Susan. "I mean, the weeds are mostly cleared—"

They skirted the gooseberry bushes, now stripped bare of fruit, to the angle of the wall where the famous peach-tree was. "Oh good," said Midge, "there are still some peaches on it."

The glorious big ripe peaches glowed against the old wall, whose yellow brick had mellowed to a soft greyish tone. Midge handed a peach to Susan and took one herself. The two girls leant contentedly up against the wall, warm in the sunshine, eating blissfully and not bothering much about the juice that was running down their chins.

"This latest craze of Charlotte's—" Susan observed, through a mouthful of peach, "this arky— whatever it is—"

"Archæology. Oh I shouldn't think that'll bother us much," said Midge, catching some juice with the back of her hand. "After all she can't bring bits of ancient Greek temples into the house like her bits of antique china and other things she has been keen on—"

"Ancient Greek temples?" said Susan, astonished. "Is that what archæology is?"

"That among other things," said Midge, who usually seemed to know things like that. "The study of antiquities, digging up past civilizations—"

Susan gaped. "How on earth would she ever get started on a thing like that?" she asked.

"Old Potter at school lent her a book out of the school library," said Midge. "She should have had more sense."

"Quite nice to dig up treasure and stuff," mused Susan.

"I don't think it's often treasure," said Midge. "Bits of broken pottery mostly, I think. Ready for another peach?"

"Och, *yes*," said Susan, "if it's all right—"

"'Course it's all right," said Midge. "We're allowed to take the fruit from this garden—"

She picked a peach and handed it to Susan and was just stretching out a hand to pick one for herself when a new and very angry voice demanded, "And what do you two think you're doing?"

Midge and Susan glanced up. A girl of about thirteen or fourteen, their own age, had come round the wall and was standing staring at them, her legs apart, her hands on her hips. She was wearing shabby old jeans and a yellow sweater; her shining black hair was cut in a fringe and caught back in a horse's tail; she had a pale creamy skin and long dark eyes. She was very pretty—and at the moment very angry. "What d'you think you're doing?" she demanded again.

"Eating peaches," said Midge. Susan gaped at her with her mouth open.

"I can see that," said the girl. "Our peaches."

Midge slowly withdrew her hand from the peach that she had been about to pick. "*Your* peaches?" she said.

"I suppose you've come from the slums of Camberwell," said the girl furiously, "and slipped in from the park on your stealing expedition!"

Susan, her Scottish blood rushing to her head, went quite red with rage and opened her mouth to return insult for insult, but Midge said calmly, "No, only from next door. And we always thought they were our peaches—"

The girl looked slightly taken aback and slightly

less angry. "When you buy a house," she said, "you usually get the peaches as well—"

"Oh help!" said Midge, making a comical little face. "You're the new people next door! Aunt Lucy wrote and told us and I completely forgot! I *am* sorry—but we've had the run of this garden for simply years and I just forgot—"

A new voice, sweet and gay, sang out, "Gabrielle! Where are you, my poppet ?"

"Here!" called the girl, "by the gooseberries—"

Another trousered figure appeared round the corner of the wall. This one was older and taller and her black hair was cut close to her head like a little cap. She wore a stained smock over her trousers. "I just couldn't work on this heavenly, heavenly day!" she cried, flinging her arms wide. "Come and be mad with me, Gabrielle my angel —" She suddenly caught sight of Midge against the wall and Susan awkwardly clutching the peach and wishing the earth would open and swallow her up.

The girl, Gabrielle, said, "Selina, these are the girls from next door—" she smiled a trifle sourly, "we've just been getting acquainted."

"Oh, but how *lovely*!" cried Selina, as if, as Midge said afterwards, she had spent her whole life looking forward to this meeting with Midge and Susan. "We've been *dying* for you to come home from that boring old school of yours, haven't we, Gabrielle ?" Gabrielle didn't commit herself. "You must be Marjorie," Selina went on to Midge. "*What* sweet name is it they call you— ?"

"Midge," mumbled Midge. She thought that if

she had never hated her nickname before, she certainly hated it now.

"And you—" cried Selina, turning gaily to Susan, "must be the little Scotch cousin—"

Susan feeling, in the midst of all this charm and gaiety as if the heather was sprouting out of her ears, admitted stolidly that she was.

"Now, *do* come up to the house for a cup of coffee or something," cried Selina, "so that we can really get to know you properly! Angélique was brewing some of her heavenly coffee as I came through the kitchen and I can't tell you how divine it smelt—"

"Yes, do—" said Gabrielle coldly.

"It's very kind of your sister—" Midge began and Selina gave her trill of merry laughter.

"Isn't it too sweet and silly ?" she said. "*Every*-body thinks I'm their sister! I'm their *mother*! And wait till you see my big son, six feet *two*! So ridiculous beside little me!" Prattling gaily on, she led the way round the corner of the wall and up the garden towards the house. The garden was much changed, Midge could now see, properly looked after, all the lovely untidy old-fashioned flowers grubbed out and showy flower-shop blooms flourish-ing in their place.

"Thanks for not cliping on us," Susan mumbled to Gabrielle in an embarrassed whisper. "You know what I mean—telling tales—"

Gabrielle looked at her coldly. "Please don't go giving me credit for some dreadful public-school virtues," she said, "because I haven't any—"

Susan was silenced.

Selina led the way into the house. This too was much transformed from its former state as a furniture store, and the room that led off the garden and had formerly been a dreary sort of cellar was now supplied with table-tennis and other large and elaborate games and its walls were gaily painted with what seemed to be a huge map of the world on to which little figures, appropriate to the country on which they appeared, had been painted. "This is our rumpus-room," said Selina. "I do think it's so important to have some tiny corner where we can make just as much noise as ever we like, don't you ?"

Midge and Susan, who were apt to be pursued into the remotest corners of their own house by an irate Aunt Lucy begging them to make less noise or the patients would hear them, agreed dubiously. "And I do think the way we've done it up is such fun," Selina rattled on. "When we get an inspiration, we paint in a little something— Look," she said, pointing to a fuzzy-looking blob with very long arms in the middle of West Africa, "Peregrine put in that gorilla yesterday, isn't it sweet ? He's gorilla-minded at the moment—when he's not busy with his silkworms, the pet. *Look* at them, munching away at their lettuce leaves—" She waved a white hand at a row of dress boxes, with holes punched in their lids.

They went up the basement stairs, the walls of which were papered in gay stripes, and turned towards the smell of coffee that was coming from a room on the ground floor overlooking the grass verges and white-painted posts of Tollgate Road, and just as Susan, who was bringing up the rear, passed the end of the staircase leading upstairs, there was a gibbering noise from above her. She turned her head quickly and a great, black, hairy *thing* jumped on her back and hurled her to the ground.

"Help! Help!" yelled Susan. "It's a gorilla! Get it off! Get it off!"

The thing released its stranglehold on her neck, darted to a corner of the hall and stood there, legs bowed, long arms curved, scratching under its arms and chattering and scolding. Susan crouched on the floor and covered her face with her hands.

"Take it *away*!" she cried.

The girl Gabrielle pulled her hands away from her face and pulled her to her feet, none too gently. She was laughing. "Gorilla!" she said. "Look at it!"

Susan looked, and the fog of terror seemed to clear away from her brain and she saw quite clearly that the gibbering gorilla was a small boy with a mop of dark curls and wrapped up in a mangy old fur jacket.

"Peregrine!" said his mother lovingly. "Terribly funny, darling, Susan thought that you were a real gorilla! We like to play these imaginative games," she added to Susan.

Susan gave a sickly grin and felt a complete fool. Not even the really delicious cakes which Angélique, who seemed to be some sort of French maid, produced and the coffee which may have been very good but was much too strong for Susan's taste, could reconcile her to this dreadful house with its dreadful inmates who jumped on you out of dark

stairways and snatched cakes out of your hand—
because the gorilla-game continued with unabated
zeal as far as the boy Peregrine was concerned.
Besides, that Selina was awful—downright silly—
Susan liked a mother to be like a mother and not
larking about like this. She thought wistfully of
her own mother, plump and comfortable far away
in Africa; she thought of darling Aunt Lucy—she
was quite young for an aunt and *very* pretty in a
careless sort of way, but she didn't get herself up
in jeans and silly-looking blouses with pictures of
vegetables on them—and Susan longed to be home.
Besides, the walls of this room would give her
nightmares if she looked at them much longer, for
they were covered with awful pictures—like those
pictures that Aunt Lucy in one of her fits of enthusiasm had wanted all the Carmichaels to hang
up on their walls—only worse. Susan gazed at one
in horror—of a—girl, she supposed it was, with a
sort of green face, sitting at a lop-sided table; and
apart from the girl's green face and dark hair, the
picture was all sort of red and muzzy.

"Are you looking at Gabrielle's picture?" said
Selina, following the direction of Susan's gaze and
fortunately not following the direction of her
thoughts.

"Gabrielle!" said Susan, amazed, looking from
the green face in the picture to the smooth olive
skin of the real Gabrielle.

"Yes, it's a Sam Pilkington," said Selina reverently.
"You know his work—of course you do, since he
lives in Wichwood, in one of those charming Millpond Cottages —he's a *great* friend of ours—"

Midge stiffened. Sam Pilkington! The very man who, Bill had told them, was trying to push poor old Mrs. Thorne out of her house! He *would* be a friend of these dreadful people! Midge couldn't wait to get out of their house.

Selina suddenly flung out her arms again with joyous abandon. "Let's dance!" she cried. Gabrielle ran to a radiogram in the corner and put on a record and, to the horror of Susan and Midge, began to dance round the room. Selina gaily dragged Susan and Midge to their feet. Hideously embarrassed, Midge and Susan thumped round like elephants.

When the record, which of course was a long-playing one, did at last stop after what seemed like a couple of centuries to Midge and Susan, Selina said, "Now I feel thoroughly refreshed! I know I could throw a superb pot—"

While the girls would have enjoyed seeing her throw pots about, they felt that this was their chance to get out of the house, so as soon as they decently could, they muttered polite thanks for coffee and cakes and took themselves off. They went charging home and ran Bill and Charlotte to earth in the old schoolroom. Bill was squeaking away on Midge's recorder and Charlotte was reading a book on archæology. Oh, the blessed peace of the shabby old room!

"Oh, give me that!" cried Midge, grabbing her recorder, "I need something to soothe my nerves! Bill, why didn't you tell us about these dreadful people who have bought number twelve?"

"I did!" said Bill. "At least, Aunt Lucy did, she

told you all about them in her letters and I wrote to you about the ghost!"

"Bill," said Charlotte, "honestly you didn't—we'd never have forgotten about a ghost—"

"Well perhaps I didn't actually write," said Bill, "but I meant to—"

"Go on then," said Midge. "Tell us now—" She settled well back in her chair, with her grubby and crumpled music-book on the arm, her recorder on her lips. The recorder was an instrument exactly to the taste of Midge, who was lazy, because you could play it more or less lying down. You didn't, as Charlotte said, even have to blow it very hard. She now began to play *Good King Wenceslas* with a lot of long pauses and an occasional high squeak.

Bill was saying, "Well of course I didn't actually see the ghost, but when the house was being put in order for these Gascoignes there were a lot of Irish workmen on the job and they saw the ghost of poor old Mr. Worthington!"

Susan was sitting up with her eyes popping. "Why should the ghost of poor old Mr. Worthington haunt the house ?" she said.

"It was his house," said Charlotte. "And he left a will saying that the house mustn't be sold, that it must stay in the family because it had been in the family since it was built in the eighteenth century. But, poor old thing, it was some distant cousin who inherited it and he didn't care whose family it stayed in and sold it right away—"

"No wonder the poor old man haunts it!" said Susan indignantly. "I do think that's mean!"

"Oh well," said Charlotte, "perhaps the distant cousin needed the money."

"Och, that's true too," said Susan.

"Bill," said Charlotte, "what was the ghost like? Clanking chains and its head tucked underneath its arm?"

"Well, naturally not," said Bill. "Old Mr. Worthington didn't clank chains or have his head tucked underneath his arm, did he? It was just an ordinary ghost in a top hat—"

"In a top hat!" shrieked Charlotte. "I don't call that a bit ordinary!"

"Och away, Bill," said Susan, "a ghost would never wear a top hat—"

"This one did," said Bill. "The workman I talked to most—his name was Pat Murphy—said he saw him quite distinctly."

Midge took her recorder out of her mouth. "Let's tell these awful people—what's their name—Gascoigne?—that the house is haunted and perhaps they'll go away," she said.

Charlotte wanted to know what was awful about the people and Midge said that the mother looked like their sister and wore jeans and was all arty-crafty and made them all *dance* round the room in the middle of the morning and threw pots about, although unfortunately she and Susan hadn't actually seen this happen. Charlotte said *honestly*, didn't Midge know anything? Throwing a pot was what you called making a vase or a pot or something like that, you *threw* it on to the potter's wheel, and this Mrs. Gascoigne was probably a sort of artist who made pots. Susan began to describe the rather embarrassing meeting with Gabrielle when Bill interrupted. "Did you meet the boy?" he said.

"Did I meet the boy!" said Susan. "He jumped on me from a great height—"

"Being a gorilla," said Midge gloomily.

"I know," said Bill. "The girl goes to one of those crank schools where they throw ink at the headmaster but the boy goes to the Prep. I had to take him up to school the first day he came and he was an Indian brave that day and went the whole way up Tollgate Road on his stomach."

"Och, yes," said Susan bitterly. "His mother likes him to play these imaginative games. One of these days," she added darkly, "I'll play an imaginative game and scare the daylights out of *him*."

"And such names!" Midge put in. "Gabrielle and Peregrine!"

"Oh, I just call him Pea-green," said Bill. "They're allowed to do what they like so that they won't get any inhibitions. He told me. Thank goodness he's only nine and in Lower II and I don't have anything to do with him at school."

Midge moved on to *Frère Jacques*, which was the other tune in her repertoire. She stopped in the middle to say, "And here's another thing—they're friends of that Sam Pilkington who wants to put Mrs. Thorne out of her house. Go on and tell us about that, Bill—"

"Well," said Bill, "you know that Mr. Pilkington has the two cottages next to Mrs. Thorne? Well, he wants to buy hers as well and make one big house."

"But surely whoever owns the cottages wouldn't

do a dirty trick like that ?" said Charlotte in horror. "Poor old Mrs. Thorne is terribly old—and besides she has lived in that little cottage for simply ages, surely she can't just be thrown out ?"

"No," said Bill, "but Mr. Hart who owns the cottage wants to sell. He's willing enough to sell it to Mrs. Thorne, but she can't afford to buy it, you see. You'll have to do something about it, Susan—"

"Bill," said Charlotte incredulously, "you're surely not *encouraging* Susan to rush in ?"

Midge stopped her mournful piping. "*Fools rush in where angels fear to tread*," she remarked to no one in particular.

Charlotte went on, "You know the trouble we've had already with Susan rushing in and rescuing people, and helping people, and poking her nose into other people's business—"

"Well yes, I know it's sometimes very uncomfortable," said Bill, grinning at Susan for whom he had a very soft spot, "but what you don't seem to realise is that once or twice she really has succeeded in doing some good—why, we shouldn't have been having this holiday in Switzerland if it hadn't been for Susan rushing in and finding that Folding Letter * which we got such a fat reward for! I mean, we've always tried to hold her back and she has got there in the end, this time I thought we ought to encourage her and she might get there a bit quicker. Because there isn't much time—Mrs. Thorne only has until the ninth of August to make up her mind—if she doesn't buy the cottage by that

* See *Susan's Helping Hand*.

date then Mr. Pilkington gets it. So you'd better get busy, Susan—"

Susan beamed at him and patted him on the head. "Och, you're a clever wee boy," she said, "and recognise brains when you see them. Of course we'll help Mrs. Thorne. Now, what shall we do?"

There was a blank silence in the schoolroom, interrupted by Midge's return to *Good King Wenceslas*. She was having trouble with the '— gathering winter fu-u-el' bit.

Susan said tentatively, "Could we give up the Swiss holiday and give all the money to Mrs. Thorne?"

"No, we certainly could *not*!" said Charlotte. "The first time we've been abroad, what an idea! Besides, Mrs. Thorne would never accept it."

"*Besides*," said Bill, the realist, "it's not *nearly* enough—Mr. Pilkington has offered a thousand pounds for the cottage."

Midge let the recorder fall out of her mouth in her amazement. "A *thousand pounds*!" she said. "Does horrid Mr. Pilkington make all that money out of those ghastly pictures? Time we took up art, you and I, Charlotte—"

"Well, I do take up art," said Charlotte. "It's the only thing I'm supposed to be able to do, draw silly little pictures—"

"Yes, but I mean make a thousand pounds out of it," said Midge. "Why don't you stop wasting your time reading dotty books about broken-down old Greek temples and draw ghastly pictures instead and make a thousand pounds?"

"Och, stop blethering," said Susan, "even if Charlotte sold every line she drew, and who would she sell it to anyway, it would take her a good wee while to make a thousand pounds and we only have until the ninth of August. No, we'll need to tackle this from the other angle—push Mr. Pilkington under a bus or something, so that he can't buy the house—"

"That's a very practical suggestion," said Midge.

"Or maybe we could persuade him to go and live in Chelsea instead," Susan went on, regardless of Midge's sarcasm. "Let's go and see Mrs. Thorne this afternoon and talk it over with her. Who is she, anyway ?"

"Don't you remember," said Charlotte, "we took you to visit her during the last hols ? We always pay Mrs. Thorne a visit, she's an old pet, she's about a hundred years old, but she does sewing and mending for Aunt Lucy—"

"We'll go and see her this afternoon," said Susan with decision, "and talk the whole thing over with her—"

CHAPTER TWO

GOSSIP—AND TALL TALES

But Aunt Lucy had other plans for the afternoon. Over the shepherd's pie at lunch-time she said, "I've made an appointment for you three girls to have your hair cut this afternoon. I don't know what they do to you at school, you're like three scarecrows. Do they cut it with sheep-shears?"

"Can I have mine washed and set at the shop?" said Charlotte. Charlotte was sixteen and inclined to have those sort of ideas now.

"Of course not," said Aunt Lucy, "spending all that money. Your hair curls in quite nicely at the ends if you don't have it cut too short. You can come straight home and wash it like the others."

"Let's all have our hair cut in horse's tails," suggested Midge, "like that Gabrielle next door—" She screwed her hair up in a knot and looked round at the others, making faces.

"You look more like a midge than ever," said Charlotte.

"Or like a skinned rabbit," said Bill. "No hair and big staring eyes—"

"There's not much I can do with mine," said Susan, shaking her dark-brown curls. "But I loathe that horse's tail style like Gabrielle's—"

"Oh, you've already met the people next door, have you?" said Aunt Lucy. "Aren't they nice?"

"Nice ?" Midge said blankly.

"Yes, of course. We thought they were a most interesting, intelligent and talented family. Mrs. Gascoigne is most gifted—she designs textiles and—"

"I expect that blouse she was wearing was one of her designs," said Midge. "Tomatoes and cauliflowers."

Susan giggled. Aunt Lucy went on, "And Mrs. Gascoigne is a potter too, she makes lovely pots, she has a workshop downstairs with a potter's wheel and everything. She was showing it to us when your daddy and I went for dinner—"

"*Daddy* went for dinner ?" exclaimed Charlotte. Dr. Carmichael never as a rule went anywhere, only tore round visiting his patients all day and half the night and sinking into a chair in a stupor of exhaustion if he happened to have five minutes off-time.

"Yes," said Aunt Lucy as if there was nothing unusual about it. "We think they're going to be delightful neighbours—"

Midge and Susan looked at each other and wondered uneasily if Aunt Lucy was going to have one of her things about the Gascoignes just when they were thinking of working up to a nice feud. Aunt Lucy and Charlotte were two of a kind, always having wild enthusiasms for something or other. "And, Charlotte," Aunt Lucy was saying, "the elder boy, Adrian, should be just your cup of tea— he's going to be an archæologist—" Charlotte's eyes sparkled. She certainly hadn't hoped for an archæologist right next door. "He's at Cambridge

—although at the moment he's with his uncle or his godfather or somebody, who is a real archæologist, on a dig in Syria—"

"On a *dig* ?" said Bill. "What's a dig ?"

Charlotte was delighted to explain that a dig was what you called an expedition to dig up archæological remains.

"You don't have to go to Syria, surely, you could dig in the garden," Bill suggested. "Old West was saying the other day that the digging was getting too much for him."

Charlotte said loftily, "You dig where you think there are interesting remains—"

"Well I'm sure there are interesting remains of all sorts of things in our garden," said Bill. "After all, it's an old house and perhaps you'll find traces of cave-men or something."

Charlotte wasn't very sure if Bill was teasing her or not. "Our house scarcely goes back to prehistoric cave-men," she said mildly.

"You'll have to ask Adrian all about it when he comes home," said Aunt Lucy, kindly but vaguely.

But Midge and Susan weren't reconciled to the Gascoignes by the promise of a budding archæologist. "Addy and Gabby and Pea-green, such names !" Midge muttered to Susan as they left the table and prepared to set off to the hairdresser's.

They were all shown into one cubicle and as usual made a grab for all the frivolous magazines that they didn't have a chance of seeing in the ordinary way. Midge was particularly lucky and got one with her fortune in it.

"Miss Brown won't be long," the receptionist

poked her head round the curtain to say. The girls didn't care how long Miss Brown was, they were perfectly happy with their magazines. The air smelt delicious with scent, the noise of a dryer was whining in the background with the voice of a customer raised above it to make herself heard.

Suddenly Susan clutched Midge's arm and nudged Charlotte to secure her attention and jerked her head in the direction of the voice. "Listen!" she hissed.

The voice, which they did not recognise, was shouting "—delightful people, so artistic, a real acquisition to Wichwood, I feel. I called on her right away—she's so young and pretty to be the mother of a family and the eldest boy quite grown-up, at the university I understand,—a widow too, tragic really—yes, I called and asked her if she would join our little discussion group, it's really quite a cultural little affair, and she agreed at once and she's going to give us a little talk on Craftsman-ship versus Mass Production and illustrate it with examples from her own work—yes, pottery—" There was an indistinct murmur from the hair-dresser's assistant, then the voice shouted again, "—I shouldn't be at all surprised if the little romance with the doctor should come to something —just next door and so suitable—"

Midge and Charlotte looked quite ill and Susan had almost crawled out of the cubicle in her anxiety not to miss a word, when Miss Brown bustled in and started wrapping Charlotte up in overalls and mackintosh capes and snipping with her scissors— and there was no further opportunity either for listening to the gossiping lady or for discussing among themselves the dreadful things she had been saying. They could only sit and brood while Miss Brown cut their hair.

They were on their way home, still pale and anxious, with their hair lank and uncomfortable against their necks, when Charlotte said with an attempt at brightness, "But of course it's all nonsense! There isn't a word of truth in it! It's only silly gossip! Daddy would never think of getting married!"

Susan cheered up at once.

But Midge said, "Well, he did go to dinner with them, and you *know* he never goes out anywhere, he's always too tired after his patients, and goes to sleep at the fire."

"Yes that's true," said Charlotte. "Oh dear!"

"We'll just need to tell Uncle Charles how awful they are," said Susan desperately. "Imagine having them in the family! That Pea-green jumping on you all day long!"

"I don't think telling him will be much good if he likes them," said Charlotte.

"How could he like them ?" said Midge.

"Well, you heard Aunt Lucy—she seems to like them all right," said Charlotte.

"*Some*how or other," said Susan with great solemnity, "we'll have to show them up in their true colours!"

"And how are we going to do that ?" Midge asked.

"Well, I don't know yet, but that's what we must do," said Susan. "Goodness, we're going to be busy —with two jobs on our hands—rescuing Mrs. Thorne and this war to the death with the Gascoignes. I suppose young Bill will be on our side all right ?"

"Oh, goodness yes," said Midge, "I can't imagine Bill welcoming Pea-green into the family as a step-brother—"

Peregrine endeared himself still further to Bill that afternoon, and by chance it was Aunt Lucy who unwittingly drew their attention to what he was doing. She was with the girls in the top-floor bathroom helping them with their hair when she happened to look out of the window.

"Oh how sweet!" she exclaimed. "There's Pere-grine taking his ducks for a walk!"

"In our garden, I suppose," mumbled Midge, whose head was in the basin, and whose speech was much impeded by a towel held in front of her face.

"Well, yes, but only in the corner of it," said Aunt Lucy, kneading strongly at Midge's head.

"I call that cheek," said Midge.

"I seem to remember that you and Susie paid a visit to their garden this morning," said Aunt Lucy.

"That was by mistake," mumbled Midge.

"Besides," Aunt Lucy went on, "we said he could let his ducks swim in our pond—they keep it nice and clean."

"Then I don't see why he should let his ducks swim on the fountain as well," said Charlotte.

"I don't know what has come over you children about the Gascoignes," Aunt Lucy, who had rather a hot temper, exploded. "There were your daddy and I thinking how nice it was for you to have a family of young people next door and you've done nothing but moan about them since you came home! Charlotte hasn't even met them yet!"

Susan, who was leaning out of the window watching the ducks, and who didn't want Aunt Lucy probing at this stage into their dislike of the Gascoignes, said quickly and soothingly, "Actually, the ducks look rather nice on the fountain. I do like ducks—look at them duck-diving away there!"

"Anyway," said Aunt Lucy, not to be mollified, "I've asked Gabrielle and Peregrine to spend a day with us this week, their mother has some pottery show on somewhere in town and it's dreary for the young people dragging round after her—"

"That French maid could look after them, surely?" said Charlotte in a sulky voice.

"Charlotte, *really*!" said Aunt Lucy.

"Aunt Lucy—" Midge interrupted plaintively, "you're pulling *lumps* out of my hair!"

Hair washed and combed, the girls went out into the garden to dry it, with towels over their shoulders. Peregrine and the ducks had gone.

"Do hurry up and get your hair dried," said Susan. "I want to go up and see Mrs. Thorne—"

"It's all very well for you," said Midge, "you can just rub up your mop with a towel and it's all dry and curly in a minute. If Charlotte and I do that we look as if we'd been pulled through a hedge backwards—"

However, as it was a nice hot sunny day, everybody's hair dried very quickly. Bill was dug out of the garage where he was making a fleet of little wooden boats. "I don't think they look too bad," he said, standing back and admiring them, "now that they're painted. I'll sail them on the fountain when we come back."

Millpond Cottages were a row of pretty little eighteenth-century cottages which looked over smooth lawns to the old millpond. The Carmichaels knew them well, because besides their old friend Mrs. Thorne, their daily help Mrs. Taylor, with her son Joe who was a policeman and a special friend of Bill's, lived in one which was tucked away at the back. The pond was lying still and beautiful in the afternoon sunshine, fringed with chestnut trees which hung their heavy branches down to the water; small children were poking titbits through the railings to the ducks.

"I don't wonder that horrid Mr. Pilkington wants to live here," said Midge as they turned off Tollgate Road to the cottages.

"Well, but if he has two cottages already what does he want with another, the greedy thing?" said Susan.

Bill was nonchalantly looking through the windows across the microscopic garden. "They must have started alterations already," he said, "I can see workmen inside—and my friend Pat Murphy —oh, I must just say hallo to him—" Bill went up the tiny flagged path and made signs through the window. Pat Murphy, glad of any excuse to stop work for a minute, lost no time in throwing up the window and leaning out to talk to Bill.

"Ye're just the very one I wanted to see, me boy-o," he said, after Bill had introduced the girls. "Here we are, working away, pulling down walls here and putting up walls there, and down in the

S.R.I. B

foundations what d'ye think we're afther finding ?"

"Buried treasure!" said Susan, ever optimistic.

"Treasure, is it ?" said Pat Murphy laughing all over his long, lean, Irish face. "Sure, and it *is* treasure, then—" he went digging into his pocket and held something out to Bill on the palm of his hand. The girls all crowded round to look and Bill picked it up.

"It's a penny!" He said. "An old penny!"

"Oh, do let me see!" said Midge. "Goodness," she said, "d'you see the date ? 1797!" They passed the penny round; it was thick and heavy with George the Third's head on it and the date.

"That's quite right!" cried Charlotte excitedly, "people used to put a coin in the foundation of the house when they built it, I read that somewhere! Fancy, these little cottages must have been built in 1797!"

Pat Murphy was delighted at the success of his little bit of treasure. "Sure and I thought you would want to see the like of that," he said.

"Oh gosh *yes*, Mr. Murphy," said Bill. "Thanks *frightfully* for showing it to us! Oh gosh, *isn't* horrid Mr. Pilkington lucky—I suppose," he added wistfully, "you'll have to give it to him ?"

"To Mr. Pilkington, is it ?" said Pat. "Begob, the penny is yours if you want it—and a small return it is for all those cups o' tay you would be bringing to us and us working next door to ye at number twelve and the weather so cold it would freeze your very breath as ye breathed it!"

Bill was sorely tempted. "Oh gosh, Mr. Murphy, I'd *love* to have the penny," he said, "but don't you think that perhaps Mr. Pilkington *ought* to have it ?"

"Mr. Pilkington," said Pat, "doesn't care a button for the penny. I showed it to him meself when he was poking his long nose into the repairs. Sorr, says I, you will be wanting to put it in a glass case for people to be looking at, says I, and he gives that laugh of his like an old billy-goat bleating, Murphy, says he, I'm not much of a one for putting things in glass cases, says he, *you* can put it in a glass case and welcome, says he—"

Bill and the girls were delighted. Not only at acquiring an old penny in such romantic circumstances, but also at finding that their opinion of horrid Mr. Pilkington seemed to be shared by this charming man. But Pat Murphy had another interesting matter up his sleeve. "Now," he said, settling himself more comfortably against the window, "ye were talking about treasure, and while it will be the sad day when the poor ould body next door is put out of her house, yet I have a great notion to get to work on the alterations because they, *say*" and he lowered his voice mysteriously "that there's a pot of money hidden away there!"

"In Mrs. Thorne's cottage!" exclaimed Charlotte. "How on earth could there be ?"

"Ah now, it isn't Mrs. Thorne's money," said Pat, "but they're telling me that the cottage once belonged to an ould miser who had the name of being very rich, and when he died, divil a bit of money did they find, so where should the money be but hidden in the house somewhere and when we start pulling it to pieces mebbe we'll find it!"

His audience digested this astonishing tale in

silence. Then Susan, looking as innocent as a baby, said, "Mr. Murphy, where would you start searching for a thing like that, now ?"

"Och," said Pat Murphy, "I've never had the good fortune to be on the hunt for treasure in the whole of me life, but I'm thinking that the place where an ould miser would be hiding his money would be behind a loose brick. Or under a floorboard would be a rale convenient place—"

"*Gosh!*" said Bill. "Wouldn't it be—"

Susan kicked him hard on the leg. "Och," she said, "I'm *very* sorry to dash your hopes, Mr. Murphy, but I don't think that Mr. Pilkington will get the house next door—"

"Sure and I hope not indade," said Pat. "Wouldn't two houses be enough for a man and him without so much as a wife or a child—"

There came an angry shout from within the cottage, "*Murphy!*"

"Ah, there's himself, now," said Pat, not stirring. "He's a darling man, the boss, but with his mind set on work all the time—"

Midge said hurriedly, before this most interesting man should be whisked away from them, "Mr. Murphy, did you *really* see a ghost down at number twelve ?"

"Indade I did!" said Murphy solemnly. "A wee ould man it was, with a beard on his chin and a top hat on his head, and he looked at me in sorrow and—"

"MURPHY!"

"Perhaps we'd better go," said Charlotte.

"And thanks *awfully* for the penny," said Bill.

They all said good-bye and Pat Murphy slowly pulled down the window which stuck fortunately and gave him another few seconds' grace before he returned to his toil. The others went down the path and had a consultation before turning into Mrs. Thorne's gate.

"Such luck!" Susan exulted.

"I suppose," said Midge in her tiredest voice, "I suppose you think that all we have to do now is prise up a floorboard and hand Mrs. Thorne a long-lost treasure and she'll be able to buy her house and everybody will live happily ever after—except horrid Mr. Pilkington ?"

"Och, who cares about him ?" said Susan.

Charlotte said, "I think Mr. Murphy is one of the nicest men I've ever met but *hon*estly, such stories!"

"Don't you think it's true, then ?" wailed Susan. "Don't you think there was ever a miser and a fortune that was never found and—"

"There may have been a miser for all I know," said Charlotte, "it's a bit before my time, for Mrs. Thorne has been in this house for quite twenty years, but can you imagine a miser's hoard lying tucked away there for twenty years waiting for us to discover it ?"

"Yes," said Susan, "I can. It would be just the thing. Very convenient."

"*Really*, Susie—" Midge began.

Bill said, "It wouldn't do any harm just to look. They all eventually agreed that it wouldn't do any harm just to look, but that Mrs. Thorne mustn't be told what they were looking for because the disappointment would be too acute if they didn't find anything, and Midge said *when* they didn't find anything. Mrs. Thorne would have to be enticed away, said Susan, glaring at Midge, and they might not be able to work it in that afternoon, but if not they'd come again the next day, with a plan; and having got so far in their schemes, they continued up the minute path and were admitted by Mrs. Thorne who had been observing them for some time from her parlour window and wondering why they didn't knock.

Mrs. Thorne was a tiny little old lady with warm brown eyes and grey hair parted in the middle and braided smoothly into a neat bun at the back. Her house was very neat and trim like herself and full of lovely old bits of furniture and interesting knick-knacks that the Carmichaels always liked to look at, such as the lion's skin hanging on the wall that her brother had once sent her from Africa. They told her that they were going to Switzerland for their holiday—the very first time that any of them had been abroad—and promised to send her a picture postcard of the snow mountains.

Mrs. Thorne smiled and thanked them. "But I don't know where I'll be by that time," she said. Her voice didn't falter, but her thin old hands worked against the stuff of her dress.

The children couldn't bear it. Bill savagely began to kick the leg of his chair, Susan's throat ached with unshed tears, Midge thought I'll kill that Pilkington, I'll *kill* him, and Charlotte burst out: "Oh, Mrs. Thorne, I'm sure something will turn up and you won't be turned out—"

"Well I'm sure I hope so," said Mrs. Thorne with

forced brightness. "Of course you know they won't really turn me out until I've found some place else to live, but my landlord does want to sell the house and Mr. Pilkington does want to buy it, so they'll expect me to move out as soon as possible. But it isn't easy to find any place to go—I did put an advertisement in the *South London Press* for unfurnished rooms, but I only had one reply and when I went to look at the house it was in a *very* nasty part of Brixton, not at all what I've been accustomed to, and although of course I can't afford to be too fussy, the house wasn't even *clean*. The trouble is that I can't afford to pay much for rent—my rent here is so very cheap—and even to find lodgings seems to be very difficult—nobody wants an old woman as a lodger. And besides, I should like to keep some of my bits and pieces with me—"

Susan and the Carmichaels were absolutely tongue-tied with misery. They wanted to rush out and bash Mr. Pilkington and the owner of the dirty house in Brixton and the lodging-house keepers who wouldn't keep a sweet old lady like Mrs. Thorne. Charlotte managed to mutter lamely, "Just got to hope—"

"Oh I do!" said Mrs. Thorne. "And I pray too, and that has never failed me yet. Now, we mustn't sit here getting gloomy on your first visit of the holidays—and I'm being a very bad hostess, have you had tea ? No, no, I'm sure you haven't, or if you have you can manage another little one—I made a gingerbread this morning, I must have known you were coming, and I'll go and put on the kettle—"

The Carmichaels and Susan all surged to their feet to help too and went out to the tiny passage that led straight through the house to the back garden which was a blaze of sun and colour framed in the cool dimness of the house. To leave this and go and live in a slum! Midge thought.

Susan suddenly pulled them back. "We don't *all* need to go and help," she said. "Charlotte, you go." She added in a fierce whisper, "Keep her there as long as poss! I have an idea—"

"Help!" said Charlotte grinning, and followed Mrs. Thorne to the kitchen.

Susan shut the parlour door behind herself and Midge and Bill. "Now's our chance!" she said, her cheeks red with excitement. "We can have a quick look round for the miser's hoard! Wouldn't it be *wonderful* to put a box of gold and money in Mrs. Thorne's lap when she comes back with the tea!"

"It certainly would be wonderful," said Midge. "Wonderful, meaning surprising—"

Susan paid no attention to her sceptical cousin. She was examining the fireplace, which framed a little gas-fire. "I can't see any loose bricks here, Bill—can you ?"

"I can't see any bricks at all," said Bill, "because they're all plastered over—we don't want to start bashing the plaster—"

"Of course we do!" said Midge. "Run next door, Bill, and borrow a pick-axe from Pat Murphy and make a job of it—"

"Och away, Midge," said Susan seriously, "we just want to have a wee keek round—"

"Talk English," said Midge. "A keek might be worse than a pick-axe for all I know—"

"Och away and don't be daft," said Susan, "a keek is a wee look—"

Bill dropped to his knees and turned back the carpet—there was no dust under that carpet—"We could have a look at the floor-boards," he said. "Pat Murphy mentioned floor-boards. And I do believe," he added, knocking and poking round the wainscot, "that there *is* a loose board here—" He felt in his pocket for his knife which he always carried for just such an emergency as this, and without too much trouble he prised up the floor-board. The cavity thus revealed was dark and dusty and seemed to stretch for a long way, beyond pipes and under the floor.

Midge sniffed. "Funny smell," she said vaguely.

Susan was delighted with their discoveries. "Just the place for a miser's hoard!" she exclaimed. "Och, but we can't see!" she said, dropping on her knees and feeling in the hole. "I *wish* we'd brought a torch—" She looked round her and jumped to her feet. "Oh good, there are matches—" She snatched the box of matches from the mantelshelf and knelt down again.

Bill, holding up the floor-boards with one hand, tried to grab at her arm with the other. "Susie, be careful!" he cried. "That pipe must be—"

But he was too late. Susan struck a match. There was a terrific explosion and a sheet of flame shot up to the ceiling.

CHAPTER THREE

SAMSON

A DREADFUL sight met the eyes of Mrs. Thorne and Charlotte when they rushed into the room. There was a gaping hole in the floor, where the force of the explosion had torn a jagged edge round the cavity where the floor-board had been; the wall and ceiling were burnt black: Susan put a hand up to her head and brought away a handful of charred hair; most of her eyelashes had gone and half of both her eyebrows, leaving her with a very peculiar and diabolical expression. Mrs. Thorne, very white, but keeping admirably calm, dabbed her face with T.C.P. and then smeared it with Vaseline, which certainly soothed the burns but didn't improve her appearance. "You might have been killed! You might have been killed!" she exclaimed.

Susan and Midge and Bill were at a loss to explain this holocaust, but fortunately it wasn't necessary, as Mrs. Thorne seemed to think it explained itself. "I've noticed a smell of gas for quite a time now," she said, "but when I tried the tap everything seemed all right. And you discovered the leak under the floor-board! I might have been gassed as I sat in my chair one night! You've saved my life, not a doubt about it! But you should never, never strike a match when you suspect a leak of gas—*you* might have lost your life instead of saving mine!"

Susan was delighted to find that she was a heroine instead of a complete fool—and she could naturally rely on Midge and Bill not to give her away to Mrs. Thorne—but there was still the question of all the damage to be faced.

"Yes, well, of course I'll have to have it put right before I leave the house," said Mrs. Thorne, looking worried. Then her face cleared, "But it's a small price to pay for our lives!"

"Oh, but Mrs. Thorne," said Midge, coming to life at last, "*we* must pay for having it put right— we did it, after all—"

Bill put in eagerly, "The workmen are next door, shall I ask the foreman to step in and give us an idea how much it would cost?"

"Yes, do," said Charlotte. She felt that she and Mrs. Thorne hadn't got to the bottom of the affair —and she hoped that Mrs. Thorne never would— but she had a very good idea how it had come about.

Pat Murphy's 'darling man' was delighted to step in. He tut-tutted over the children's escape and said that there was nothing in the repairs—a five-pound note would cover the whole thing, decorations and all.

"A five-pound note," said Susan, feeling sick. She hadn't five pence, let alone five pounds.

Charlotte explained that the bill must be sent to them and the foreman agreed in spite of Mrs. Thorne's protests. "You won't be able to do it just at once, will you?" said Susan hopefully, but the foreman assured her heartily that it wouldn't be too long, when the men were working next door anyway they could just nip in and put the damage right and it might work in a bit cheaper that way. Susan felt that it would have to work in a good lot cheaper before she'd be in a position to pay for it, but they all beamed on the foreman in a falsely hearty sort of way and said that that would be splendid.

They cleared up the mess as best they could and begged Mrs. Thorne not to go catching her heel in the jagged hole and spraining her ankle or anything like that, and Mrs. Thorne fed them on tea and gingerbread to restore their shattered nerves, and they said good-bye and went sadly home again. Aunt Lucy was given an edited version of the affair with all mention of misers' hoards left out and agreed, though she felt sorry for them, that it was only right that they should foot the bill as Mrs. Thorne was quite unable to pay out five pounds for an unnecessary expense at this, or indeed any other, time. "And perhaps it will be a lesson to you, Susan, not to go near an escape of gas, *ever*, with a match—you might have been seriously hurt."

Susan was too much chastened even to ask Aunt Lucy if *she* had ever heard tales or rumours of a miser having lived in Mrs. Thorne's wee cottage, and they all trailed out into the garden.

"It's a fine beginning to our schemes to help Mrs. Thorne," said Susan. "Try to help her buy her house and run her in for a bill for five pounds!"

The girls thumped down on the grass in the corner of the garden that was still sunny, under the apple-tree beside the fountain. "Maybe we'll have to tackle it from the other angle after all," Susan went on. "Ill-wish Mr. Pilkington—or something."

"Heavens," said Charlotte, "don't let's start getting mixed up with black magic. Natural forces seem to give you enough bother, Susie."

"I ill-wish horrid Mr. Pilkington all the time," said Midge, "but I don't seem to have the right recipe because nothing happenes—not to horrid Mr. Pilkington anyway. You don't think we should take Susie off the job, do you, Bill ?"

Bill didn't answer. He had fetched out his fleet of boats and was preparing to sail them on the pond. He was lying across the little rockery, doing it no good at all, peering into the rather murky depths of the water. "What's happened to all my goldfish ?" he said. "Flash is here and Spotty, but I can't see James and Timmy with the Telescopic Eyes and Golden Streak—"

"Oh it's awfully difficult to count goldfish," said Charlotte. "They dart about and you think it's one you've counted. It's not easy to recognise goldfish."

"It's easy to recognise Timmy with the Telescopic Eyes," objected Bill. "You can't mistake him, his eyes stick out about a mile. Do come and help me count—"

The girls obligingly got up and lay on their stomachs across the little rockery. There was a good deal of discussion and cases of mistaken identity and claims to have seen Timmy with the Telescopic Eyes, but in the end it seemed all too true that there were only two goldfish where there ought to have been five.

"I don't understand it," said Bill. "It's very worrying. Where can they have gone ? They were all there this afternnon when I gave them their ants'-eggs."

"This afternoon!" said Midge slowly, sitting back on her heels. "Bill, do ducks like goldfish?"

"Well of course they do," said Bill, "it's their favourite food, practically—"

"Then," said Midge solemnly, "I think I know where your goldfish are, old boy—they're inside Pea-green's ducks!"

"Oh, of course, these blessed ducks!"

"Brought them over on a string to feed off your fish!"

"And we all stood there and watched them!"

The girls all exclaimed together.

Bill gave a roar of rage. His goldfish, reared and watched over with such care, gone to make a meal for Pea-green's ducks! Bill was for dashing next door that instant in order to execute rough justice. In other words, "I'm going to wring their necks!" he said. "And then Pea-green's—!"

Midge admitted that that was certainly what he must feel like, but that she was sure that wringing a duck's neck was a lot more difficult than you would think, not to mention Pea-green's.

At dinner, Uncle Charles and Aunt Lucy, Susan thought, were a lot less sympathetic than you would expect about the goldfish. Uncle Charles quite frankly laughed, while Susan and the younger Carmichaels sat with stony faces, and Aunt Lucy laughed a little too and said, "Oh, poor little soul! He can't have known that ducks eat goldfish!" But it wasn't Bill she was talking about—it wasn't Bill who was the poor little soul, but Pea-green.

"Don't you believe it," Susan muttered. "That Pea-green knows everything—" and after dinner she told Bill not to worry, *she'd* help him to be revenged on Pea-green—she didn't quite know how, but she would think of something . . .

Next afternoon, Aunt Lucy was planning to take them up to town to buy some new clothes for Switzerland. And, said Aunt Lucy, who seemed to have repented in the night of her lack of sympathy, they would go to the pet-shop in Harrod's and get Bill a couple of goldfish if they weren't too expensive. Bill said rather broodingly, thanks very much, it was very kind of Aunt Lucy to think of it, but he'd never get another goldfish like Golden Streak or Timmy with the Telescopic Eyes, and did Aunt Lucy think he ought to keep the pond filled with goldfish just for Pea-green's ducks to feed off ? And Aunt Lucy said that if they mentioned it—politely— to the Gascoignes, she was sure it wouldn't happen again, and his name was Peregrine.

"*Peregrine!*" said Bill expressively.

When they had come home after a very successful shopping expedition and Charlotte was with Aunt Lucy helping with dinner, Midge took her recorder and went out to the garden with Susan. Bill had put his two new goldfish, not yet christened, which he had been persuaded to accept, into the pond and was sitting by it with a book and a water-pistol at the ready. He had wanted to buy an air-gun at Harrod's toy department, but Aunt Lucy had always set her face against such weapons and this time was no exception. Midge and Susan grinned at him and

went on their way to the orchard, for the rest of the
family were apt to be unsympathetic when she was
practising her recorder, especially Bill, who himself
had a very nice singing voice. Bill had made up a
poem about it—he had once had ideas about being
a poet, but that was before he turned his attention
to engineering and ship-building. It was just as
well that he had the girls thought when they heard
the poem:—

My sister is a born musician,
But when she plays I try not to listen.
It is on a recorder she does play,
'Over the hills and far away',
And makes a most unholy row
Rather like a sea-sick cow.

She keeps me up for half the night
Trying to make a tune go right,
But all she does is squeak, squeak, squeak,
And so like that for all the week.
But I must confess I'm not any better,
And when I try to play her tunes
She very, very nearly swoons.

Midge said that there was a line too many in the
second verse, and Bill said that he couldn't help that
—that was what was called poetic licence.

The girls settled themselves comfortably with
their backs against an apple-tree and Susan thought
of plans for getting rid of the Gascoignes before
Uncle Charles married them, and helping Mrs.
Thorne, and didn't listen to Midge much except

when an especially ghastly note made her draw in her breath sharply. Gradually, another sound penetrated her consciousness—somebody seemed to be delivering a sermon, or spouting poetry or something she thought. She cocked her head and listened—it made a change from *Good King Wenceslas*, anyway.

> "O indignity, O blot
> To honour and religion! servile mind
> Rewarded well with servile punishment!
> The base degree to which I now am fallen,
> These rags, this grinding, is not yet so base
> As was my former servitude, ignoble,
> Unmanly, ignominious, infamous,
> True slavery—"

Eventually Susan's curiosity got the better of her, never a very difficult feat, and she rose and went and looked over the fence. Peregrine was on the other side of the fence, practically on the Gascoigne's compost-heap; he had hung up a cheap looking-glass on the fence and was hacking at his black curls with an enormous pair of kitchen scissors.

Susan gasped and he looked up and saw her. "I wish you would be quiet," he said, "I very nearly cut myself then—"

"You wish *I'd* be quiet!" said Susan in a high squeak. "What about you, spouting away at a lot of rot!"

"That's not rot," said Peregrine, "that's *Samson Agonistes*. Milton, you know," he explained kindly.

Susan had heard of Milton, of course, but she didn't think that anybody knew bits of him off by heart, except that carol '*Ring out, ye crystal spheres*', which was jolly nice. "Well, I wish you'd be quiet," she said, "it's the most awful row—"

"I can't be quiet," said Peregrine, "because I *am* Samson—"

"You are ?" said Susan.

"Yes," said Peregrine. "And," he said, hacking off an extra large lump of black hair, "it's extremely difficult being Samson and Delilah at the same time. Do come over and be Delilah for me—"

"I don't feel much like being Delilah," said Susan, "she wasn't a person I ever cared for. But," she said, looking at him, "I do think somebody ought to help to tidy you up a bit before your mother sees you—"

"Why ?" said Peregrine.

"Well," said Susan, "she'll have a stroke—"

"Of course she won't have a stroke, "said Peregrine scornfully. "She lets us do what we like, I told you." He looked appraisingly at Susan and added, "You don't look too wonderful yourself. Do you always look as awful as that ? Do you never have any eyebrows ?"

Susan said with dignity, "I met with an accident."

"Oh," said the odious boy, obviously sorry to have missed that. "Well, you can come over and tidy my hair if you like—"

Susan didn't particularly like, but she did want to talk to Peregrine and she always liked to have a finger in any pie that happened to be around, so she climbed over the fence. At close range his hair style was even worse than it had seemed from the other side of the fence. All the glossy black curls had gone, rough jagged spikes stood up all round his head, interspersed with bare patches where he had apparently pulled chunks out by the roots. Round him on the compost-heap lay his shorn locks.

"It seems to be too far gone to do much," said Susan, "but anyway, here goes—" She took the scissors, although shears, she thought, would be better name for them, and gingerly began to tidy up the head of the shorn Samson. "And keep still," she said, "or I'll jab the scissors into you. I'll do that anyway," she added, "unless you promise never to bring your ducks to our pond again to eat Bill's goldfish—"

Peregrine was all injured innocence. How was he to know that the ducks would eat the goldfish until it was too late and they had? His ducks were used to that pond, they liked it—"I'll bet they do," Susan put in—they always used to come over with him when he came for tadpoles in the spring.

"Did you often come for tadpoles?" asked Susan, thinking now that it was a miracle the goldfish had lasted as long as they had.

"Quite often," said Peregrine carelessly. "I sold them to the chaps at school. Ten for a penny."

"Our tadpoles!" said Susan furiously.

Peregrine shrugged. "Nobody else seemed to want them," he said.

Susan told herself grimly that it was quite time that this awful Pea-green was taken down a peg or two. "Pea—gr— I mean, Peregrine," she said in an off-hand voice, "did you ever hear that your house was haunted ?"

"Haunted ?" said Peregrine. "By a ghost, d'you mean ?"

"Naturally, by a ghost," said Susan. "Did you ever hear that ?"

"I don't believe in ghosts," said Peregrine. "Selina never allows us to read ghost stories or fairy stories or anything like that."

"I thought you were allowed to do anything you liked," said Susan, nicking his right ear a fraction and hurriedly mopping up the blood with her handkerchief.

"Be careful," said Peregrine severely. "Not bad things like fairy stories," he went on.

"Fairy stories aren't bad!" cried Susan furiously. "Have you never been told the story of Cinderella ?"

"Never," said Peregrine. "It's all lies."

"So is your silly old *Samson Agonistes* all lies!" said Susan. "And dull too—"

"'Tisn't," said Peregrine smugly. "It's immortal poetry."

"Well, maybe it is," said Susan weakly, "but Cinderella is jolly nice too—not that *I* read fairy stories now, of course," she added, as she didn't want Peregrine to have the wrong idea of her.

"You should try Milton one day," said Peregrine, "although acherly I'm not sure if you're quite mature enough for Milton—"

Susan thought that she was mature enough to strangle this odious boy, and that in one minute she would do it, but she managed to swallow her rage. She snipped in silence for a moment or two. "This ghost I was telling you about," she said, "that haunts your house—don't you think you and your family would be frightened to live in a haunted house?"

"I don't see why, when we don't believe in ghosts," said Peregrine reasonably enough.

"But people have *seen* him!" said Susan, exasperated.

"What people?"

"A workman who was doing up your house for one, before you came to live here," said Susan. "*He* saw the ghost. It's the ghost of old Mr. Worthington who used to live in your house and he haunts it because he doesn't want you to live in it."

"That's just too bad," said Peregrine calmly. "What's he supposed to look like, this ghost?"

"He's a little man," said Susan, delighted that at *last* the fish seemed to be nibbling the bait, "with a beard and a top hat—"

Peregrine began to giggle, to the imminent danger of the back of his neck. "Who'd be frightened of a silly old ghost in a top hat?" he said.

"Well," said Susan indignantly, "*I* would, for one!"

At that moment she heard a gasp, and she looked up to see the gay and charming Selina, no longer gay and charming but trembling with rage, staring at them in horror over the compost heap.

"You—you—you *murderess*!" she cried in a terrible voice. "What have you done to my baby's hair?"

"Oh hallo, Selina!" cried Peregrine. "Isn't it fun, she's cutting my hair! I'm Samson and she's Delilah!"

"I—I—" began Susan, lowering the shears. At the same moment Midge, disturbed in her practising by the raised voices, popped her head over the fence. She goggled at the sight of Peregrine and Susan with the shears in her hand.

Mrs. Gascoigne was nearly crying with rage. She grabbed the scissors out of Susan's nerveless hand and flung them down; she seized Peregrine in one hand and Susan in the other and began dragging them through the little tumbledown gate that led to the Carmichaels' garden. "Come with me!" she cried, like a tragedy queen, Midge said afterwards. "Until I show your aunt and uncle what you have done to my child!"

"I—I—I—" said Susan.

They met Aunt Lucy at the back door, hanging out some stockings to dry. Mrs. Gascoigne stormed and ranted and pointed to her boy and covered her eyes with her hands while Peregrine hung his head —to hide a grin as a matter of fact—and kicked at a tuft of grass in the yard and Susan stood like a fish, opening her mouth and saying nothing, supported by Midge, who had tagged along behind and who had nothing to say either. Finally Mrs. Gascoigne, after one last wild look of hatred at Susan, put her handkerchief to her face and ran towards her own house and Peregrine, now quite solemn again, gave a little sort of formal bow to Aunt Lucy, said good afternoon and followed his mother.

"Susan!" said Aunt Lucy aghast. "How could you ?" And at that moment Dr. Carmichael drove into the yard in his car.

"What on earth's the matter with little Mrs

Gascoigne ?" he asked, joining the group. "I saw her dashing into her house looking very upset. And Peregrine—has he got ring-worm, d'you suppose ? He looked as if he might have—"

Aunt Lucy gave the best explanation she could of the situation, and Uncle Charles turned to Susan. "Susan!" he said in his turn. "How *could* you ?"

"Well," said Susan helplessly, finding her tongue at last but still battered by the storm that had broken over her innocent head, "well, he asked me to—"

"Susan, really!" said Aunt Lucy, beginning to lose her temper. "If he'd asked you to hold his head under the pond would you have done it ?"

"You bet!" muttered Midge under her breath.

"I'd better go over there right away and apologise," said Uncle Charles, harassed. "Susan seems to have taken leave of her senses. I'll talk to you later, Susan," he said over his shoulder and strode off.

Susan swallowed. Uncle Charles was the most perfect darling and hardly ever cross, but—"Beware the anger of a patient man," Midge murmured in her ear, but if she imagined that she was being helpful, Susan thought, she was being anything *but*.

Aunt Lucy went on hanging out her stockings and Susan did her best to explain what had happened between her and Peregrine.

"So you were only trying to tidy it up a bit for him ?" said Aunt Lucy eventually.

"And telling him ghost stories to while away the time," put in Midge, again *sotto voce*.

"Yes," said poor Susan with a gulp, "I mean, you

think he looks awful now, but you should have seen him before I started on him. A gollywog with the mange is the only way I can describe it—"

"I hate boys with curls, anyway," said Midge.

"Yes well, I don't suppose his mother will quite agree with you, Midge—nor with the methods for getting rid of the curls," said Aunt Lucy, "but perhaps when she has cooled down a bit—oh dear, and I did so hope that you and the Gascoignes would get on nicely together!"

But when Uncle Charles came back he seemed quite jovial. "Mrs. Gascoigne was extremely nice about the whole business," he said. "Some kind of game, she said, Susan had apparently persuaded him to play Samson and Delilah although I must say I should have thought that Susan was beyond that sort of thing, and she supposed, though I don't imagine it's likely, that Peregrine was almost as much to blame as Susan, for he's such a bundle of mischief. And Lucy, she has asked us to go with her to the theatre to-night, and I said I thought we could—Mrs. Taylor will sit in, won't she? I'm quite looking forward to it," he added, "I haven't been to a theatre since the pantomime at Christmas. It's the New Group Theatre—you know that little highbrow one in Chelsea and it's a friend of Mrs. Gascoigne's who wrote the play—she's sorry it's such short notice but he only sent her the tickets this afternoon."

"Goodness," said Aunt Lucy, "they've got interesting friends, the Gascoignes! We only seem to know doctors and schoolmasters and bank managers and an odd stockbroker. I'd better go and send

Mrs. Taylor home now so that she can give Joe his supper and be back to let us out—" and Aunt Lucy and Uncle Charles went into the house quite cheerfully.

Midge and Susan looked at each other in disgust and went to wash their hands for dinner.

CHAPTER FOUR

THE GHOST OF MR. WORTHINGTON

IT WAS a very depressed little company that sat out after supper, when the grown-ups had taken their departure. There was a little sort of terrace with a half-wall round it outside the drawing-room window, and leading on to the garden, and they sat there, enjoying the scents and coolness of the evening, but not enjoying their thoughts much.

Susan gave a gusty sigh. "We have had two perfectly awful days," she said. "The most dreadful things have happened and all we have to show for it is that Uncle Charles has gone to the theatre with That Woman, we've let ourselves and Mrs. Thorne in for a five-pound bill and I've lost my eyelashes." She felt the charred stubs tenderly. "D'you think they'll ever grow again?"

Midge said helpfully, "I read in one of those magazines at the hairdresser's—help, was it only yesterday? What a lot we've been through since then,—that castor oil makes your eyelashes grow."

"What, drinking it?" said Susan in horror.

"'Course not, you dope," said Midge. "Rubbing it on—"

"Och, I wouldn't mind that," said Susan. "D'you think that Uncle Charles would give me castor oil to make my eyelashes grow?"

"I expect he would if he had any—you don't need

to tell him what it's for, after all," said Midge, "but he won't have any unless he has had a sample sent and I shouldn't think anyone would send him a sample of castor oil. Don't you know that the only medicine we've ever had in our lives has been free samples sent to Daddy? It's a wonder any of us are alive."

Charlotte was sitting with a pencil bending over a small drawing-block because the light was getting so bad. "Who d'you think that is?" she asked, holding up the horrific result.

"Struwwelpeter," said Bill.

Susan giggled. "Pea-green, of course," she said. "Exactly like him, the little beast. Bill, did you know that he has been selling *our* tadpoles to boys at school for ten a penny?"

Bill was speechless with rage at the thought of this source of revenue that had slipped through his fingers.

Charlotte said, "Wouldn't you just love him for a dear little brother?"

There were loud groans from the others and Midge said, "Don't *talk* about it, you'll give me nightmares. Don't you think we ought to point out the danger we're in to Aunt Lucy?"

"Och, but she seems to like them," said Susan.

"Well, perhaps she does," said Midge, "but she'll lose her job if Daddy marries again—looking after us, I mean."

"Maybe," said Bill tragically, "maybe she wants to lose it! Maybe she's tired of looking after us!"

Susan's eyes filled with tears at the very idea, but no one else seemed to think that this was very probable. But then grown-ups were queer, of course, Midge added, you couldn't tell, sometimes, what they would like.

This gloom was really becoming too intense for Susan. "Don't worry," she said with an assurance that she was far from feeling, "I'll think of something."

"I wish you wouldn't, Susie," Midge murmured plaintively.

"Och, I know things haven't gone too well to-day," Susan admitted humbly, "but we'll show these Gascoignes in their true colours to Uncle Charles yet—"

"Unrelieved black," said Midge.

"Uh-huh. And meantime, we ought to be thinking how we're going to raise five pounds to pay Mrs. Thorne's repairs."

"I wish I could find some wonderful arky-whatever you call it treasure like Charlotte said," said Bill. "I wish I could dig somewhere—"

"Well, not in the garden, ducky," said Midge hurriedly, following the direction of Bill's glance.

"It's an old house," Bill mused on, "and the foundations can't have been disturbed for years—"

"It's too late to-night," said Midge firmly. "It's practically pitch-dark."

Charlotte said witheringly, "You don't find archaeological treasure in back gardens. You find it at Mycenæ or on the site of Troy or Babylon or in Crete or among the ruins of ancient Byzantine cities—"

Nobody knew what she was talking about. Bill said again obstinately, "Well, it's an old house—"

"Listen," said Charlotte. "This house is about two hundred years old and the ruins that Sir Arthur Evans found in Crete were six *thousand* years old— four thousand B.C."

"Help," said Bill, "that makes me feel quite tired."

"I'm not surprised," said Midge, "considering that it's long past your bed-time. In fact, we'd better all go in, and Bill, you'd better go to bed."

They went in and shut the french windows against moths and other flying creatures, but did not draw the curtains. Bill busied himself with a lot of things that had suddenly become urgent, to stave off the hour of bed. Charlotte found her book on archæology and prepared to settle down for a little read. "You two had better be making tracks for bed too," she said in rather an elder-sisterly sort of way to Midge and Susan, "it's late. Give me a shout when you've had your bath, Susie, and I'll put some more stuff on your face—"

Charlotte's ministrations as a nurse were well known to the family and equally dreaded by them. "Poor old Susie," said Midge. "You'll lose the rest of your eyebrows."

Susan did not even laugh; she was staring at the uncurtained window. "I thought—I thought I saw something—" she said doubtfully.

"What sort of a thing?" said Midge. "A bat?"

"A face," said Susan.

Midge quickly glanced at the dark window at which Susan was staring. Bill put down his little wooden battleship and stared at Susan. Charlotte gave a little shriek and dropped her book. "*Hon*estly, Susan," she said, bending down and picking it up, "you gave me such a fright. I thought you said a *face*!"

"I did," said Susan. "I just sort of caught a glimpse of it out of the corner of my eye."

There was a moment's uneasy silence. "Let's put out the light and look," said Midge.

"Well, I *couldn't*," quavered Susan. "I'd absolutely die!"

"Let's tell Mrs. Taylor, then—she'll soon send him packing if he's a tramp."

"I don't think it was a tramp," said Susan. "It was sort of—green!"

Nobody spoke. Then Charlotte laughed a slightly forced laugh. "*Hon*estly, Susan—" she said.

Midge said, "Hadn't we better put the lights out and see what this funny thing of Susan's is with its green face ?"

Everybody felt quite brave except Susan, although she, as she hastened to point out in her own support had some excuse because she was the only one who had seen it. They put out the lamps and stared into the garden, which gradually lightened from impenetrable black as their eyes became accustomed to the darkness. The girls and Bill, in spite of their bravery, huddled together. Susan was quite frankly clutching Midge's arm. They could hear the sound of Mrs. Taylor's iron thumping comfortably in the kitchen as she ironed some things for Aunt Lucy.

"How long," Midge murmured, "do we sit here ' like birds in the wilderness ' ?"

"Oh well—" Charlotte began,—and suddenly they saw it, suddenly it loomed up from nowhere and came up to the window, a face with a queer shining light over it—and a *beard*? It came closer still to the window and pressed its face against the glass. It was indescribably horrible to see that queer unearthly green face pressed against the glass, its nose splayed out and its lips distorted and squashed flat.

Susan's nerve broke. "Help, help, it's *coming in*!" she yelled.

But the face drew back a little and a faint, unearthly, dreary voice moaned, "Revenge! Revenge!" and the face became fainter and fainter, and the voice became fainter too. "Revenge! Revenge! Revenge!"

In a breathless whisper Bill said, "Look! Look there by the gate where the light catches it! It's got a top-hat on!"

"Well of course," said Susan in a desperate sort of voice, "because it's Mr. Worthington's ghost!"

"It has come to the wrong house, surely," said Midge, in a valiant effort to make a little joke, but you could tell by her voice, Susan thought thankfully, that she was scared to death too.

"Bill, can you still see it?" said Susan. She couldn't see herself because her eyes were tight shut and had been for some time, ever since the dreadful face had been pressed up against the window.

"Yes," said Bill. "It's standing by the gate into the yard. I can see it quite plainly—the top-hat and the—"

And then quite suddenly Bill seemed to take leave of his senses. He darted to the french windows and began to unfasten them. As the others exclaimed,

Susan opened her eyes. "Bill!" she shrieked. "Don't open the window! Don't let it in!"

"If it's a ghost," said Bill, struggling with the catch which Aunt Lucy was always meaning to have mended because it was awkward and usually caught people's fingers, "then a window won't keep it out. But if that's a ghost, then I'm a Dutchman!"

"But Bill!" said Susan. "It's Mr. Worthington's ghost—it has a top-hat on!"

"Yes!" said Bill. He opened the window at last, darted out and called over his shoulder, "Yes, but it's got shorts on at the other end!"

"Shorts?" said Susan. "Shorts? I'm going dotty!" She turned distractedly to Charlotte who had stumbled across to the table and switched on the lamp. "What is he *talking* about?" she said.

Charlotte was running out of the window too. "*Charlotte!*" said Susan, "don't you go after the ghost too!"

"Ghost my foot," called Charlotte softly. "It's Pea-green!"

Susan thought that she would burst with rage. To think of them all in that room absolutely *stiff* with terror; to think of that dreadful face pushed against the window, the squashed nose, the livid lips—and it was Pea-green all the time! "But what was that green look on his face?" she said.

"Luminous paint, would you think?" said Midge. "Come on," she said, "let's go and strangle that odious child."

They rushed out through the window—slap bang into Charlotte and Bill who were in a huddle by the edge of the little terrace. Susan lost her head slightly and began clutching at Bill, and would have hurled him to the ground, given any encouragement. "All right, all right! It's only me," whispered Bill. "We've lost him! I saw him slip down the side of the lawn towards the fountain, but now I've lost him—"

"I expect he's making for home through the back gate," Midge whispered. "Can't we head him off?"

"You and Charlotte go round by the lane and try to catch him before he reaches his own garden. Susan, you come with me—we'll go down towards the fountain."

Susan would rather have gone straight upstairs to bed, but she was too ashamed of such feeble-mindedness to say so, therefore she followed Bill meekly as he skirted the lawn and went towards the fountain and the old summer-house. "No one here," he whispered, peering in. They went round the fountain and under the apple-tree. Bill put his mouth to Susan's ear and whispered, "Wait here. I'll nip through the little gate and see if the others have caught sight of him—"

"Leave me here?" quavered Susan.

"Yes, I shan't be a minute." And he glided away.

Susan thought that she would never have come if she'd known she was going to be left all alone in a pitch-dark garden under an apple-tree waiting to catch a ghost that wasn't a ghost but was just as bad—worse, really; she'd rather meet a ghost on a dark night than Pea-green, she was sure of that And what was that funny noise going on above her head—a rending, tearing sound, and then a steady

C

munch, munch, munch? She couldn't make it out. She looked up into the branches of the apple-tree, and saw it—a great green face, disembodied among the leaves, and it was eating apples.

Then everything happened at once. Susan yelled, "He's here! He's here!" Bill and the girls appeared from nowhere. The green face dropped down out of the tree and slipping between them streaked across the lawn; Mrs. Taylor called out, wanting to know where everybody was and what all the yelling was about; then she caught sight of the green face and added to the yelling herself; everybody bumped into everybody else and tripped over each other and Susan fell in the fountain.

Charlotte stamped her foot with rage. "He's gone!" she exclaimed. "We'll never catch him now! And to-morrow he'll deny the whole thing!"

"What's worrying *me*," said Bill glumly, hauling a dripping Susan out of the fountain basin, "is whether my new goldfish will ever survive a visit from Susan . . ."

The telephone bell at the Carmichaels' house rang so often in the middle of the night, that long ago everybody had become conditioned to it and slept peacefully through it—except presumably Dr. Carmichael. But this night had been so alarming, so disturbed, and Susan was sleeping so badly on account of it that when the telephone bell shattered the silence of the night it shattered Susan's fitful slumber too. She jumped out of bed and, putting on the light, ran to the top of the stairs. The telephone must have wakened Aunt Lucy too—

perhaps Uncle Charles had been tired after his un-accustomed night-life and had let it ring for a long time—for she poked her head round her door and spoke to Uncle Charles, who came out of his room with a coat and trousers over his pyjamas.

"It's young Peregrine," he said in answer to Aunt Lucy's sympathetic mutter. "Screaming night-mares, and poor little Mrs. Gascoigne can't do a thing with him and is in a state about his inhibi-tions, not to mention a nervous breakdown. Appar-ently Susan has been filling his head with some story about the ghost of Mr. Worthington. I shall," he added, in rather a grim way, "be having a word with that young woman in the morning—"

Susan was so indignant that she went back to the room she shared with Midge and wakened her. Midge was a sound sleeper, and very much disliked being wakened in the morning, far less in the middle of the night. She glared at Susan, bleary-eyed.

"Listen to this!" spluttered Susan furiously. "That odious child has screaming nightmares because I was telling him ghost stories! *And* that woman thinks he'll get inhibitions and a nervous breakdown!"

"That odious child hasn't a nerve in his body," said Midge sleepily. "If he has screaming night-mares it's on account of stuffing himself with green apples. Although," she said, lying down again and tucking the sheet round her, "I jolly well hope he *gets* inhibitions—and gets them badly . . ."

CHAPTER FIVE

BURIED TREASURE

UNCLE CHARLES started on his few words with Susan
at breakfast next morning. Midge didn't like telling
tales, but she was not going to sit back and shield
Pea-green at the expense of Susan.

"The fact of the matter is, Daddy," she interrupted
as soon as she could, "Susan may have mentioned
about Mr. Worthington's ghost to that Pea-green,
but it was Pea-green who came last night with
luminous paint on his face and a top-hat on his
head and nearly frightened the life out of *us*. It's
a wonder that *we* haven't all inhibitions this
morning."

"You seem to have the vaguest idea about inhibitions," said Dr. Carmichael. "Fortunately,
perhaps—"

"What's this about Pea-g—I mean *Peregrine*,
frightening the lives out of you?" said Aunt Lucy.
"Mrs. Taylor said that there had been some shem-
ozzle but I couldn't make head or tail of her
story—"

Her nieces and nephew told her. "And *if* he had
nightmares," Midge finished, "it was from eating
little green apples. Our apples."

Dr. Carmichael, that unfeeling man, roared with
laughter. "I must say," he said eventually, "that
my own diagnosis of Peregrine's trouble was unripe
apples."

"This is the day," Aunt Lucy reminded them, thinking a slight change of subject was indicated, "that Gabrielle and Peregrine are coming for lunch."

"Oh no!"

"Oh help, Aunt Lucy, not *to-day*!"

"Did we not have enough of him last night?"

"And that sneering, stuck-up Gabrielle!"

"I have a lot of things that I particularly want to do to-day—and entertaining Pea-green isn't one of them—"

"Darling Midge," said Aunt Lucy mildly, "when did you ever want to *do* anything? Now, not another word, I simply don't understand the way you children seem to have taken a dislike to the Gascoignes—I think they're very clever, original, intelligent and amusing children who—oh, my *goodness*!" She stopped her eulogy of the Gascoignes in mid-sentence and clapped her hand to her mouth as she hastily read the letter that she was holding in her hand.

"Not bad news, I hope?" said Bill politely. "That Pea-green's too ill to come, f'rinstance?"

"*That* wouldn't be bad news, you dope," said Susan.

"No, no," said Aunt Lucy, "nothing like that—it's only that I promised to make sweets for Mrs. Mountford-Jones's garden fête and it's on Saturday and I forgot all about it! It's quite six months since she asked me, and of course I promised anything, it seemed so far away, and now here it is, on Saturday!"

"There will be a few over for us, won't there?"

said Bill, already smacking his lips for Aunt Lucy made the most heavenly sweets from Scottish recipes—stuff called tablet that was divine, and Helensburgh toffee which was a sort of tablet too, and Russian toffee and treacle toffee, her speciality, which she made from black treacle.

"Oh goodness, I shouldn't think so," said Aunt Lucy distractedly, "I promised to make *ten pounds*! Here, have a look at the leaflet, it tells you all about the fête." As if she was going to make the sweets that minute, she stuffed her last piece of toast in her mouth and got up. "Oh, and don't forget to tell the Gascoignes about the fête—they might like to come and I told Mrs. Mountford-Jones that I'd bring as many people as I could—"

There were rebellious mutterings and angry murmurs from the family. They couldn't even enjoy a fête without these Gascoignes, it seemed. Dr. Carmichael went off to collect his bag and his list and start his rounds. Bill and Charlotte, whose turn it was, began half-heartedly to clear the table, Chang came in, raucously demanding his breakfast, and Susan quickly fetched his saucer and put down some milk for him at which he turned up his nose because he wanted liver or at least bacon, which he could smell quite distinctly. Midge sat on at the table, getting in the way of the clearers, and read out the attractions at the GRAND GARDEN-PARTY AND FÊTE to be held in Mrs. Mountford-Jones's beautiful garden which was at the corner of Tollgate Road and Wichwood Common. "*Tennis, Croquet, Fish-pond, Treasure-hunt*—that's one for Charlotte—oh I say, listen to this! *3 o'clock*—

Fancy Dress Parade, *First Prize* £2. Two pounds! If one of us won that it would help with Mrs. Thorne's bill!"

"It certainly would," said Bill, pulling the cloth off the table and scattering a few crumbs in Midge's lap. "But why should one of us win it ? I expect there'll be hundreds of entries."

"If we were original, clever, intelligent and amusing like the Gascoignes we might win it," said Charlotte, "as it is I never can think of a thing to wear at a fancy dress."

Midge said, "Here's something else! EXHIBITION OF HOME CURIOSITIES. *Have you some interesting or curious articles in your home? Send it to the exhibition and win £5. Entrance Fee 2/6 !*"

"Well," said Bill, "we've got Susan, could we enter her ?"

"Och away, Bill!" said Susan, throwing a table-napkin at him. "Be serious! This is our chance! Surely we've got something curious and interesting in the house that we could enter! I mean, five pounds!"

"You keep thinking we'll win," said Charlotte plaintively, "but I can't imagine why we should."

"Well, it gives us fresh hope, don't you think ?" said Susan.

"False hope," said Charlotte.

Another little event that was interesting—at least for Susan—occurred while she and Midge were washing the dishes. For the telephone rang and after Aunt Lucy had chatted for some time she called Susan.

"It's a Mr. Dean," she said, putting her hand over

the mouthpiece, "he's a South African, knows your Mummy and Daddy—"

Feeling quite excited, Susan took the telephone from Aunt Lucy. "Hallo," she said.

"Oh hallo," said the strange voice, "is that Susan ? Well, I saw your mom and dad a couple of days ago—they saw me off on the plane—and they're very well and send lots of love—"

"A couple of days ago!" said Susan. "Where are you speaking from, then ?"

"London," said Mr. Dean. "Incredible, isn't it ? I still feel slightly dazed myself. I arrived here yesterday and I've been down to Southampton already to fetch my car—"

"You actually saw Mummy and Daddy two days ago!" said Susan, hardly able to believe it and feeling for the first time that her parents weren't so far away after all.

"Yes, and I have some photographs for you and a little parcel. Miss Carmichael has very kindly asked me to dinner on Friday, so I shall see you then and give them to you—"

Susan went back to her dish-washing in quite a flutter of excitement.

"Mean dodger," said Midge. "Fine time to be running off to the telephone when you're supposed to be helping me wash the dishes. Who was it, anyway ?"

"Well, it was this Mr. Dean, I think his name was, and he saw Mummy and Daddy the day before yesterday! Think of it, only the day before yesterday and he reached London yesterday! And he's coming for dinner to-morrow and he's got a parcel for me—"

"Oh, good show," said Midge, who adored parcels, even somebody else's.

"Oh, Midge," said Susan, "supposing there was something very curious and strange in the parcel, like the—like the—dried skin of a black mamba or something and we could send it to the exhibition!"

"Where d'you think Aunt Margot would get the dried skin of a black mamba?" asked Midge.

"Och, I don't know," said Susan. "It was just the strangest and most curious thing I could think of on the spur of the moment."

"And the nastiest, I should think," said Midge.

It was another lovely hot summer's day. There had been a faint mist early in the morning which had cleared away in the hot sun; the dahlias and asters were a blaze of colour in the garden. Aunt Lucy finished her domestic chores and started to make the sweets, already the most heavenly smells were coming from the kitchen. Charlotte went off to see her friends the Greenwoods; Midge took her recorder, her music, a book and a rug and went drifting to the orchard to spend a morning after her own heart—doing practically nothing. She persuaded Bill to go down the village and buy a bar of chocolate for her, and Susan said that she would go with him.

"Get me some salad stuff for lunch, then," said Aunt Lucy and gave them a basket.

Wichwood Village was lovely, just like a real old village, although it was now a part of London, with little shops and old gracious Georgian houses, grass

verges on the road with white posts and railings
round them and chestnut trees shading the pave-
ment.   Susan and Bill sauntered along.   They
looked in the book-shop window, as they always
did, and bought the lettuces and things in the
greengrocer's at the corner, and the greengrocer
gave them each a bunch of grapes; he was a kind
man like that, always giving them a little tit-bit
when they went into his shop, they liked him very
much.   Then they bought Midge's bar of chocolate
and wondered if they should have one between them
and then decided better not, even a sixpence could
ill be spared with Mrs. Thorne's repair-bill looming
over them.   "We'll make Midge share," said Bill.
"Where did she get the money anyway ?   She said
that she was flat broke until Saturday—"

On the way back they met Mrs. Thorne, neat and
trim as usual in a grey dress and a black straw hat
with a bunch of cherries on it, coming down the
village to do her shopping.   Her news was no better,
slightly worse, if anything, for horrid Mr. Pilkington was urging her landlord to make up his mind
and sell right away, so that he could get on with
the alterations before the beginning of winter; but
fortunately Mr. Hart had said no, he had promised
to wait until the ninth and he *would* wait until the
ninth and in any case Mr. Pilkington would just
have to have patience because he wasn't going to
put Mrs. Thorne out of her house until she had
some place to go.   Bill said that he thought that
was more cheerful news, couldn't she just never find
any place to go, but hang on indefinitely ?   And
Mrs. Thorne said no, she wouldn't like to stand in

her landlord's way because he wanted the money, she knew, and besides, it was very uncomfortable with Mr. Pilkington glaring at her under his bushy eyebrows every time they chanced to meet. Susan said that she wouldn't give a button for horrid Mr. Pilkington's eyebrows and Mrs. Thorne mustn't worry—which reminded Mrs. Thorne to ask Susan how *her* eyebrows were and Susan, who couldn't be bothered with eyebrows just then, said that they were *fine* thanks, and wouldn't it be wonderful if Mrs. Thorne managed to buy the house under horrid Mr. Pilkington's nose and could say sucks to him ? Mrs. Thorne's lips quivered for an instant, and then she blinked and smiled resolutely and said oh well, something would turn up, she was sure. She had put an advertisement in the toy-shop window, but of course, she had to admit, no matter how it turned out, it was unsettling.

When Susan and Bill had got back to the house and had talked Midge into sharing her chocolate with them, Bill took Susan aside.

"Susie," he said, "about this arky-business, I don't care *what* Charlotte says—her and her old Crete city that's six thousand years old—how does anybody know, anyway ?"

"Well, she explained that," said Susan. "Dates and things are known in Egyptian history and they compare the things found in Crete with Egyptian things and find their date that way."

"It's kind of fascinating, too," said Bill, screwing up his face and thinking of things that were six thousand years old. "I shouldn't mind being an arky-whatever it is myself. And that's what I was going to talk to you about. How about you and me having a quiet dig here all by ourselves?"

"Och, Bill, *yes*!" said Susan. "Och, I'd like that fine! And if we find something, such bliss! Will I get Midge?"

"What good d'you think Midge would be on a dig?" asked Bill. "Can you picture Midge digging?"

"Well, no," Susan admitted. "Unless with a teaspoon, maybe."

"A teaspoon's no good to us," said Bill. "Come on—"

He first of all led Susan down to the cellars—not a very inviting place, where Aunt Lucy kept her jam-jars and where Charlotte had once tried to grow mushrooms during one of her rare periods of horticultural enthusiasm. The cellars stretched quite a long way under the house and one of them, now empty, had racks for wine-bottles, and was very dark and creepy. But all of them had firmly con-creted floors.

Bill shone his torch round gloomily, "This isn't much good," he said. "We'd need a pickaxe and I can't see Aunt Lucy letting us bash away at the cellar floors with a pickaxe, can you?"

Susan said no she couldn't. "A pneumatic drill's what we want," she said, "but I don't know where we'd get one."

Bill said that he didn't think Aunt Lucy would like a pneumatic drill any better than a pickaxe, and led the way up into the outer air and the bright sunshine again, which Susan liked better anyway for it was cold and shivery in the cellars.

They stood at the back door looking round and wondering where to begin their dig. The yard was paved, so *that* was out, which was just as well. There were two little flower-beds under the kitchen and consulting-room windows, but Bill didn't fancy them much—Aunt Lucy or Mrs. Taylor would be popping out every five minutes to find out what was going on. They went into the kitchen to see if Aunt Lucy had any saucepans ready for scraping, and she had, so they had a blissful time scraping out coconut tablet. They saved a little for Midge and Charlotte on a saucer and then went back to their dig.

"If only we knew where to dig," said Bill. "With all the garden to choose from and the orchard as well—"

"*I'd* think nearer the house, wouldn't you ?" said Susan. "Let's go round to the front seeing that Aunt Lucy's busy in the kitchen."

There were flower-beds round the front windows too, but Bill thought that was too public a place to dig—people passing along the road would look over the hedge and ask them what they were doing.

"Well, here—" said Susan, pointing to a bush of winter jasmine under the dining-room window. "It's kind of at the side and if anybody looks at us we can saunter down the side of the house to the yard and pretend to be looking for something."

Bill wasn't very sure. "This wing of the house is a newer part," he said. "It was built on to the Georgian bit in the middle only about fifty years ago—"

"Well that's all right," said Susan, "perhaps we'll

get down to the foundations of a previous house, an Elizabethan one or a Norman keep or something— or even to the Georgian bit if it came along as far as this."

Bill said that it was treasure rather than foundations that he was interested in, but they had to start somewhere, he supposed, so they might as well start here, and the ground looked nice and soft, only they must be careful of the winter jasmine because it was lovely when it was in flower. He went off to the garage and brought back a couple of spades. He said that they were the lightest that he could find—but they still looked very heavy to Susan.

They felt heavy, too, and digging turned out to be a jolly lot more tiring than she had imagined. They dug and dug for simply ages, and she had blisters on her hands and the hole still wasn't very big when she decided that she had had very nearly enough. She straightened her aching back and thumped her spade down into the hole. There was a slight jar and a sound that was a little bit different from the previous dull thuds as her spade struck something in the earth. "Och," she said, leaning on her spade, "I'm *dead*."

But Bill said, "Didn't you hear that?"

"Hear what?" said Susan.

"A sort of clonk," said Bill, "when you stuck your spade in—"

"Oh *Bill*!" said Susan. "D'you think we've found something?"

"Well," said Bill, dropping to his hands and knees

and peering into the hole, "I suppose it might be a stone—"

"Oh, no it isn't!" cried Susan positively. "It's a treasure!" And she picked up her spade again and leant over.

"Careful! Careful!" exclaimed Bill, grabbing the spade that Susan was preparing to plunge into the hole. "We have to be frightfully careful—Charlotte read it out of that book—we might do irr—irrep— a lot of damage at this stage if we bash away with spades, we might shatter a priceless pot! We must clear the earth away with our hands."

"Okay," said Susan agreeably and she went down on her hands and knees and plunged her arms into the hole and dug with her fingers at the spot where her spade had struck, and brought up to Bill's amazed sight a long thin object, covered with mud. "Och," said Susan, "only an old kitchen knife!"

Bill took the knife from her and scraped away the mud. "Well, I don't know, Susie," he said, "it's a funny looking knife. Not like any of ours. Look at the pointed blade and that bit coming across between the blade and the handle—our knives haven't a bit like that. It looks more like a dagger to me!"

"Oh Bill!" breathed Susan. "Do you honestly think so? Oh how blissful, oh Bill, have we really found an ancient dagger?"

CHAPTER SIX

AN AFTERNOON WITH THE GASCOIGNES

THEY QUICKLY filled in the hole and rushed up to the orchard to find Midge; and rather to their surprise, Midge was very impressed. When Charlotte came back from the Greenwood's just before lunch she was impressed too. So was Aunt Lucy, but she was rather distracted with her sweet-making and the Gascoignes coming to lunch to appreciate it properly. "It's really thrilling," she said, "but show it to me later when I can have a proper look— I wondered if you'd like to have a picnic-lunch by yourselves up in the orchard—there's cold ham and salad and stuff, and apple tart and meringues for pudding and I can put lemonade in a bottle—"

The family thought that this would be better than sitting in the dining-room on such a hot day with Aunt Lucy drooling over Pea-green and Gabrielle and annoying everybody. So Aunt Lucy made them all change into clean dresses and Bill into a clean shirt because of visitors, and Bill and Charlotte carried up the food, and Midge sat down again under a tree, playing her recorder. Susan hung about waiting for Peregrine and Gabrielle and then led them up through the garden to the orchard. Gabrielle was again in shabby jeans and grubby shirt, as she had been the first day they had met her and Peregrine was frankly filthy from head to toe— so *they* hadn't taken much trouble over their appearance, Susan thought, but probably changing to go out to lunch would give them inhibitions.

As they approached the picnic party under the apple-tree, Gabrielle suddenly grabbed Susan by the arm. "What's that ghastly noise ?" she said.

Susan said coldly that it was Midge playing her recorder.

"Good heavens," said Gabrielle.

"She has only just begun to learn it," Susan said defensively.

"I don't think she should bother to go on," said Gabrielle. "Fortunately I brought my little portable radio," she continued. "We can play that."

It was on the tip of Susan's tongue to say furiously that she'd rather have Midge's recorder *with* all its squeaks and wrong notes than Gabrielle's horrible wireless-set, but she couldn't help being intrigued by the small black and cream box that Gabrielle was carrying. "Is *that* your radio ?" she said, nodding at it.

Gabrielle held it up. "Yes," she said off-handedly, "rather neat, don't you think ? Selina gave it to me for my last birthday."

Susan gaped. "A wireless-set! For your birthday! I suppose," she said cautiously, "that these neat little ones cost rather a lot—"

"Well of course I don't know what it cost, but I should think about fifteen pounds," Gabrielle said carelessly.

Susan gasped and then hastily tried to swallow her gasp—she would not like the Gascoignes to think that she was impressed. "What did you get, Pea-gr—Peregrine ?" she asked. "A TV set ?"

"No," said Peregrine seriously. "We're getting that for Christmas."

Midge's dismal notes stopped abruptly the minute that Susan appeared with Gabrielle and Peregrine. But as Charlotte was spreading the cloth and laying out the food and being introduced to Gabrielle and Peregrine, Gabrielle stretched out a casual hand and picked up the recorder. "D'you mind?" she said to Midge and without waiting for an answer she put it to her lips and tootled up and down a scale then slid into a delightful cool little tune.

When she had finished none of the Carmichaels said anything, but Susan, speaking as if the words were choking her, said, "Goodness, you play awfully well. What is that called?"

"I call it *Green Thoughts*," said Gabrielle. "You know that bit from Marvell—

Annihilating all that's made
To a green thought in a green shade—

Susan certainly didn't know that bit from Marvell, but she wasn't going to let the Gascoignes know. "What d'you mean, *you* call it *Green Thoughts*—?" she asked.

"Well, I made it up," said Gabrielle, handing the recorder to Peregrine who had been clamouring for it rather rudely ever since Gabrielle had stopped playing.

"I suppose you can play Beethoven's *Fifth Symphony* on it?" said Charlotte in a sweet voice.

"Well of course one wouldn't, on a recorder," said Peregrine scornfully and played a part of the *Nutcracker Suite* with much fluency and spirit.

Susan could see that Midge was longing to break

her recorder over first Peregrine's then Gabrielle's head, so she quickly said the first thing that occurred to her, "Are you fond of music and—and—poetry and all that ?" she said. "Like Marvell and *Samson Agonistes* ?"

"Of course," said Gabrielle, tossing her horse's tail. "Decent music and decent poetry. Don't forget I go to a decent school where one gets a chance to appreciate good stuff. I suppose you learn *Winnie the Pooh* and things like that ?"

"I *like Winnie the Pooh*," said Susan, quite red with anger. "I liked him when I was six and I still like him. I laugh like anything every time I think of him stuck in that rabbit-hole—"

"Really ? " said Gabrielle.

"Well," said Charlotte quickly, fearing for Susan's blood-pressure, "let's eat."

Lunch went off quite well, except that Peregrine started with meringues and apple tart and finished with cold ham and salad. "He always eats that way round," Gabrielle said.

"It's really much more sensible," said Peregrine in his high, pedantic voice, "because then you eat the interesting things first, when you're *really* hungry and can enjoy them—"

That's all right, thought Bill crossly, because then you have room for six meringues and leave none for me. I hope you have inhibitions all afternoon, you greedy little beast.

And the time after lunch went quite well too, because Susan, who thought she would rather listen to the B.B.C. than to that stuck-up Gabrielle, drew attention to Gabrielle's tiny radio and begged her to let them hear it. Gabrielle switched on. Bill took Peregrine off to climb trees and explore the pond and kindred delights. "Try and drown him," Midge whispered savagely, under cover of Gabrielle's fiddling with the nobs.

"The only *slightly* disappointing thing about my little set," said Gabrielle, "is that it's difficult to get the Third Programme on it, although I can always get that on Selina's. And there are often some quite good talks and music on the Home—"

"Oh, there's ' Listen with Mother', do let's hear that, I haven't listened to that for ages," cried Susan, terrified that Gabrielle would switch on to some awful talk on Milton or somebody like that and then expect them all to understand what it was about.

"' Listen with Mother' is great fun," said Gabrielle, surprisingly. "I always listen to it. In fact," she added before Susan could work in a crack about *Winnie the Pooh*, "I keep meaning to write some stories for it and send them in—"

"D'you write stories as well as tunes ?" asked Charlotte.

"Oh, nothing much," said Gabrielle smugly. "School magazine of course, and although I says it as shouldn't, our magazine is of a frightfully high standard. And I've had a couple of things published in *Young Adventurer* and a script broadcast in Children's Hour—"

"These potty little stories would be a bit beneath you then," said Midge. "I should think they're frightfully easy to do."

"I *don't* agree with you," said Gabrielle. "I think

they're extremely difficult—to keep them simple without talking down to the little dears—"

"Well, I think they're too simple," said Midge—just to be different, Susan supposed, for she didn't imagine that Midge knew the first thing about it—"I'd like something more exciting to happen."

"Why don't we all write a story for fun and send it in and see who's right?" exclaimed Gabrielle, looking round gaily and reminding Susan very strongly of Selina.

"Write a story?" said Susan. This girl was absolutely off her rocker. Write a *story*! Not for prep or anything! For *fun*!

"Let's do it now," said Midge.

Susan looked at her as if she too had gone off her rocker, but Midge's answering look said well, isn't it better than making conversation? Charlotte politely but firmly declined to have anything to do with writing stories you didn't have to on hot summer afternoons, and Susan said that she couldn't write a line to save her life, she always got C at school for her essays and would have got D only there wasn't such a mark. "I'll take the plates and things in," she offered, "and bring back pencils and paper."

She met Aunt Lucy, who gave her a plateful of Russian toffee to hand round. Susan told her that they were being clever and original and intelligent and amusing in the garden with Gabrielle—in fact they were writing stories.

"You too?" said Aunt Lucy, flabbergasted.

Susan giggled and said no, she was just fetching paper and pencils, and Charlotte wasn't. and Bill wasn't nor that Pea-green, in fact, only Midge and Gabrielle were. They were hoping that it would keep Gabrielle quiet, she said, and slid off before Aunt Lucy could think of an answer to that one.

The afternoon slipped peacefully away. Midge scribbled off a story about a dragon whose favourite food was odious little boys. As these characters were based on Peregrine she enjoyed herself very much. Then she went to sleep. Gabrielle wrote busily for simply ages, then confessed that she had done two stories. Charlotte wakened Midge and demanded that the authors should read aloud their efforts. Gabrielle immediately obliged and everybody—genuinely—thought that they were very good, only rather dull.

"Now you, Midge," said Charlotte.

"Read it out?" said Midge, and blushed. "I couldn't!"

So Susan read it out, as well as she could for laughing and Midge's bad writing and Charlotte grabbed a piece of paper and began drawing dragons all over it to illustrate the story. Only Gabrielle didn't seem to think that it was screamingly funny, which wasn't surprising, Susan thought, because she obviously had no sense of humour whatever.

"I'll type them on Selina's typewriter," Gabrielle offered, "and then we'll send them in. Selina has a friend in the B.B.C.—she'll pass them on for us, I know."

Then Aunt Lucy came to call them in for tea, and when they were having tea she mentioned the fête and they all started talking about what they should wear at the fancy dress, and nobody seemed to have any ideas except Midge.

"I'm going as a scarecrow," she said. "It's nice and easy to do, just Daddy's old clothes and bottle straws for my legs that I can get from Mr. Jones at the off-licence in the village, and a broomstick through my sleeves—"

Peregrine, who had left the table without so much as by your leave as soon as he had eaten his way backwards from cake to bread-and-butter, now went poking round the dining-room, even opening drawers and having a quiz inside. He picked up Bill and Susan's knife which was on the sideboard. "What's this?" he asked.

"Och, just an old knife that Bill and I happened to find," mumbled Susan, who didn't want to talk about their archæological discoveries to the Gascoignes.

"Oh, but that looks interesting!" said Gabrielle. "Tell me about it."

Susan reluctantly muttered that there was nothing to tell, that Bill and she had just happened to dig it up.

"Do let me take it and show it to Selina!" said Gabrielle. "She loves anything like that, and she knows a lot about old things too—she'll probably be able to tell you what it is."

Susan and Bill were furious. They wanted their dagger to themselves, to gloat over and to show to Uncle Charles; but with Aunt Lucy there they were obliged to be polite and to wrap it up in a piece of newspaper and let Gabrielle have it; it was small consolation that she and Peregrine took themselves home with it quite soon.

"I'm exhausted!" said Midge. "I'm going to lie down. That's the longest, dullest, most boring afternoon that I've ever spent—"

"Not only dull but nasty," said Charlotte, and rushed out of the room with Susan before Aunt Lucy's wrath could burst upon them.

CHAPTER SEVEN

KITCHEN KNIFE, *circa* 1920

AFTER DINNER and after Bill had gone upstairs to bed, the girls helped Aunt Lucy to wrap up her toffee and tablet and put it into little bags; then they tottered upstairs feeling slightly bloated with all the odd crumbs of coconut tablet and misshapen bits of toffee that were not good enough to go into the bags and went into their mouths instead. Charlotte came into the bathroom for a chat while Midge and Susan were having their bath and sat on the dirty-linen box with her drawing block and pencil, drawing dragons.

" You're obsessed with dragons," said Midge.

" Well they're rather fun to draw," said Charlotte. " Besides, I've got an idea."

" What sort of an idea ?" said Midge, lazily soaking in the bath with her eyes shut.

"Tell you later—if it comes off," said Charlotte and drew exciting-looking flames issuing from the mouth of her dragon.

Susan, soaping herself vigorously, said, "I have an idea too. How would it be if we sent our dagger to the exhibition of Home Curiosities ?"

"That's not a bad idea," said Midge. "Only shouldn't we need to say what it was—*Eighteenth century dagger found in a garden in Wichwood* or whatever it is."

"But we don't know what it is," objected Susan.

Charlotte said slowly, "D'you know, I believe the Victoria and Albert would tell us. I remember that when I was interested in old china somebody told me that the Victoria and Albert would identify pieces for you—they wouldn't ever say what they were worth, but they'd tell you their date and if they were genuine antiques or fakes or whatever—"

"Who on earth are Victoria and Albert?" said Susan. "Fancy them knowing all about china and would they know about daggers too?"

"Victoria and Albert Museum, you dolt," said Midge.

"Och, a *museum*!" said Susan. "Och, Charlotte, we *couldn't*! We couldn't take our wee knife up to a *museum*! They'd laugh at us—"

"Well, that's what I've been told," said Charlotte. "And Midge, isn't it about time you got out of that bath?"

Midge said, "Get out? I haven't even washed yet." She made no attempt to do so but lay still. "I think it's worth trying," she said. "After all, they can only say no. And the Victoria and Albert's always good fun to visit—and Susan has never been, have you, Susie?"

Susan said no, but she didn't think a museum was exactly her idea of fun.

"Well, the Victoria and Albert *is* fun," said Charlotte. "Heavenly china and old toys and clothes— We could go to-morrow morning."

"We haven't got the dagger," said Midge.

"Oh, we can pick it up on our way to the station," said Charlotte. "Yes, do let's do that—and maybe

Aunt Lucy will give us money to have ices in Harrod's."

"Any money we can screw out of Aunt Lucy had better go in the kitty for Mrs. Thorne's bill," said Susan. "But do let's go to this museum if you think they won't throw us out."

Aunt Lucy, when they asked her in the morning at breakfast, was quite in favour of their going too. "But will you give me a hand first?" she asked. "Remember, Mr. Thingummy is coming for dinner to-night—"

"A visitor for dinner?" said Bill. "Oh good, that means decent food."

Aunt Lucy, who was always apt to lose her sense of humour if the children cast aspersions on the food, began to say, "Bill, *really*, isn't the food always—" when Dr. Carmichael butted in.

"Why don't we ask little Mrs. Gascoigne for dinner as well if this Mr. Thingummy is coming?" he said.

"Yes," said Aunt Lucy in a considering voice, "that's quite a good idea and it would pay her back for the theatre, only if she comes, then the children can't have dinner with us because we only have six of the good Cypress lace mats—"

"Well," said Dr. Carmichael, "I don't know that the children should stay up for dinner anyway—" There was a subdued roar of protest from the 'children'—really, what a dreadful father he was turning into! "And if they do," Uncle Charles went on, unmoved, "haven't we a table-cloth?"

"Well, I only thought they should be there because of his talking to Susan about her mother and father," said Aunt Lucy. "And I did want to use the good mats because he's a famous author."

"A famous author!" exclaimed Charlotte.

"Yes, he's the man who wrote *Crime on the Congo* and then they made a film of it. I read it ages ago, but I've forgotten all about it, even who did the murder, and I wanted one of you to pop down to the bookshop and see if Miss Brown had a copy—"

"You might have told us," said Charlotte.

"I forgot," said Aunt Lucy guiltily.

"Well," said Uncle Charles, "all the more reason for having Mrs. Gascoigne. You can make dinner half an hour later and he can talk to Susan before-hand."

After breakfast Charlotte said furiously, "The very first famous author we've had and we have to eat in the kitchen while That Woman sits in the dining-room and talks to him!"

"We'll get the same food, Charlotte," Bill said soothingly. "Aunt Lucy said so."

"Besides," Charlotte went on, "he's Susan's really. If her people hadn't given him an introduction to us he wouldn't be here—oh, I do think it's so unfair!"

"For goodness' sake," said Midge, "he might be a dreary old bore and half an hour will be enough. And I thought we were going up to the Victoria and Albert? We'll miss the 10-20 if we don't hurry up—"

They were just ready to depart for the 10-20, thinking that they were in nice time to walk comfortably to the station for once, when Aunt Lucy called them back to put hats on, and of course as usual Midge couldn't find hers.

"I'll go and get the dagger from Gabrielle," said Bill. "That should save a bit of time."

Midge said, scrabbling about in the bottom of her wardrobe, "When That Woman becomes our stepmother we'll be able to go out in our filth and up to town without hats, that's one consolation."

Susan felt quite ill at the dreaded word *stepmother*, and Charlotte made angry noises. "I'm sure it's unlucky even to mention the possibility," she said. "I say, here's your hat, on this shelf!"

"Goodness," said Midge, jamming it on her head, "where it ought to be! I'd never have thought of looking there—"

Meantime Bill had rung the bell of number twelve and asked the French maid for Gabrielle. He couldn't make out what she answered, but she went away and a minute or two later shock-headed Peter appeared. "Gabrielle has gone up to town," he said.

"Oh gosh!" said Bill. "Oh well, Pea-green, see if you can find our dagger that she took away last night, there's a good chap."

"Certainly," said Peregrine in his pedantic way, "I know where it is, I'll get it."

The girls came running out of their house, past the gate of number twelve. "You go on," called Bill. "He's getting it. I'll catch you up—"

Peregrine came back with the knife wrapped up in its newspaper. "Oh thanks a lot," said Bill. He thrust it into the inside pocket of his jacket and ran up Tollgate Road after the girls. He caught them up in the lane that crossed Howletts' Mead.

"It would—be nice—" panted Midge, "if just

once—in a while—we left in time—for the beastly train and we could *walk*—along this lane—and look at the squirrels—and things. I've *never* walked along this path—always jog-trotted—feeling I'm going to burst!"

They heard the train as they reached the station, but with a superhuman effort they tore up the ramp and the stairs and reached the platform just as the gates were about to clang shut.

"Just made it!" they gasped, grinning at the porter, who was an old enemy of theirs, one much given to slamming the gates in their faces, so that they watched their train depart from behind frustrating bars.

"Hey!" called the porter. "Wot abaht yore tickets ?"

"We'll get them—at Victoria—" Charlotte panted over her shoulder as she pushed the others into a compartment.

Bill was all for going to Harrod's first, getting a copy of Mr. Dean's book and spending the money that Aunt Lucy had given them for elevenses. But the girls were firm. "Business before pleasure," said Susan grimly.

"Oh, the Victoria and Albert won't be as bad as all that, Susie," said Midge, grinning at her.

When Susan saw the imposing entrance to the Victoria and Albert, she wanted to go home. Even the others quailed a little. They walked round the museum a good deal, looking at the toys and the old china—in honour of Charlotte's late enthusiasm —before they screwed up enough courage to tackle an attendant and tell him what they wanted. But when they finally did so, it did not seem to surprise the man in the least.

"A knife, you say ?" he said. "Well, our Mr. Tebbutt's going off to a meeting at half-past eleven, but if we're quick we'll perhaps just catch him." While Bill kindly explained how the dagger had come into their possession, the man led them up and down stairs, past offices with closed doors, to private-looking premises into which the public seldom penetrated, until they came to a door with ' our Mr. Tebbutt's ' name on it.

Bill fished the parcel out of his pocket and handed it over to the man, newspaper and all. The attendant knocked, and when a voice told him to come in, he disappeared.

Simmering with excitement, Susan and the Carmichaels looked at each other.

In a minute or so the man came out, grinning. "Kitchen knife," he said, "*circa* 1920," and held out the knife in the newspaper.

They were stunned. They just couldn't believe it. They had been so *sure* that the knife was old an interesting and perhaps even valuable. Susan said brokenly, wondering if there was a ray of hope there, "What does *circa* mean ?"

"It means *about*," said Charlotte.

Bill reluctantly held out his hand to take the knife. Funny, his eyes were all blurry and he couldn't see properly. He looked down at their poor little knife, blinking hard. Then he said sharply, "This isn't our knife!"

"Here," said the attendant, not grinning now, "what are you trying to say, young feller ? Think the Victoria and Albert is trying to pinch your kitchen knife *circa* 1920 ?"

The girls crowded round looking down at the knife, which indeed was a perfectly ordinary old knife like the one Aunt Lucy kept for peeling potatoes, with a thin worn blade, and the ivory handle broken and worn away.

"That's nothing like our knife!" said Susan.

Charlotte said to the attendant before he lost his temper irretrievably, "Of *course* we don't think you pinched our knife, but is that the knife we gave you ?"

"Yes," said the man, "it is."

"Well," said Midge grimly, "we know where *this* knife came from and I suggest that we go straight home and stick it in her. Come on."

They surged off. Charlotte stopped behind long enough to thank the attendant, to apologise for giving all that trouble for nothing, and to explain as best she could that the knives had been switched. The others, having no idea of the way out, had after all to wait for the attendant, feeling silly.

They had no inclination now to go and eat ice-cream, all they wanted to do was to get home and murder Gabrielle; but when they called in at the Gascoignes' house in passing, the French maid told them that Gabrielle was still out.

"Let's spend the afternoon meditating revenge," said Midge.

"Well, I promised to do the flowers for Aunt Lucy," said Charlotte, who was good at that sort of thing, "but I can meditate as I do them."

Susan said grimly, "We're going to tell Uncle

Charles about it, aren't we ? I don't like telling tales, but I do think it's our duty to show him what kind of people they are, and when it comes to stealing, well that's just a bit too much."

Everybody agreed, but there was no time when Dr. Carmichael rushed in at a quarter to three for lunch and his two o'clock surgery, but when he reappeared at six and fell exhausted into a chair, Susan and the Carmichaels gathered round him solemnly. They were all clean and tidy and changed ready for Mr. Dean's arrival, and Dr. Carmichael opened his eyes and smiled at them. Charlotte wondered miserably if he would be smiling when she had finished what she had to say, but she would just have to chance that—it was for his own good, after all.

"Daddy," she said, "I'm afraid that I have something rather nasty to tell you about the Gascoignes, about Gabrielle anyway. I'm very sorry to have to tell you this about your friends—"

Dr. Carmichael looked mildly surprised. "I should rather have thought that they were your friends," he murmured.

"—but I don't know if you'll count them as friends," Charlotte went on, regardless of this manifestly ridiculous interruption, "after you hear about this—" and she went on to tell him about the knife that Susan and Bill had dug and how Gabrielle had taken it to show to her mother. "And we were sure," Charlotte said, "that it was an ancient and interesting knife, so we asked for it back and we took it up to the Victoria and Albert to ask them about it—you know—and when we got there we discovered that Gabrielle had kept our knife and given us back a horrid old kitchen knife, *circa* 1920—!"

"Well, you would look silly," said Uncle Charles grinning, "taking an old kitchen knife up to the Victoria and Albert—"

Susan's bosom swelled with rage. Was that all Uncle Charles had to say? Honestly, she thought, he must be simply be— be— what was the word?— *besotted* about those beastly Gascoignes when he could hear of them robbing and humiliating his own children and niece and only grin about it—!

"But *Daddy*—" Charlotte was beginning again indignantly, when the bell rang.

"Oh help," said Uncle Charles, struggling out of his chair, "here's our famous author and I haven't even washed—!" But instead they heard the gay voice of Selina saying to Aunt Lucy, ". . . you do look nice! Pet of a dress—!" and Aunt Lucy replying, "This old rag? It's at least ten years old," but she sounded pleased all the same, and Mrs. Gascoigne said, "I put on this little thing I got in Paris," and she came in, looking *chic* and exquisite in a simple black dress that made Aunt Lucy's pretty frock look like something she'd picked up at a jumble sale.

"Well of course I can't apologise *enough* for coming so dreadfully early! You must hate me—" she said, shaking hands with Dr. Carmichael, and perfectly confident that everyone would be delighted to see her no matter when she came. "But I just had to dash in early and *apologise* for my naughty Peregrine —*did* you hear what he did, Dr. Carmichael?

Wrapped up a dreadful old kitchen knife and gave it to Bill instead of his own lovely, *fascinating* knife—" and she laughed merrily and glanced round at the stony faces of Susan and the Carmichaels and you could *see*, Midge said afterwards, that she was congratulating herself on the fact that she at least had a sense of humour even if these lumps next door hadn't. "And he *completely* spoilt my little surprise," Mrs. Gascoigne went on, pouting charmingly, "so that now I must tell you about it—Susan, I do absolutely think that your knife is really old, eighteenth century perhaps, but to make quite, quite sure Gabrielle took it up to a friend of ours in the British Museum who knows just everything there is to know about old English household things—he was away to-day, but he's going to let me have it on Monday."

"Oh," said Susan blankly. "We wanted to enter it in the exhibition of Home Curiosities at the fête to-morrow—! But thanks all the same," she added grudgingly.

"Oh my *dears*!" cried Selina. "Now you *do* hate me! *What* a muddle I've made! And poor little me thinking I was doing such a good thing!"

"And so you were," said Uncle Charles heartily. "Very kind of you to go to all that trouble and bother with the children's bits of nonsense, wasn't it, Charlotte?"

"Very," said Charlotte dutifully. "Thank you very much, Mrs. Gascoigne."

Midge couldn't bring herself to speak. As soon as she decently could, she jerked her head at Susan and they slipped out of the room, followed by

Charlotte and Bill. She stood in the hall, glaring at the drawing-room door behind which Mrs. Gascoigne was chattering gaily to Dr. Carmichael.

"Foiled again!" said Midge in a very melodramatic way. "We haven't the knife for the exhibition and Daddy still likes That Woman! It doesn't matter what we do, these horrible Gascoignes get the better of us!"

Susan's round cheerful face was full of gloom. "Och, I could kill her!" she said. "Our wee knife! Bang goes five pounds towards Mrs. Thorne's bill!"

"Well, to be fair," said Bill, "we might *not* have won the prize, but," he said, moodily kicking the leg of the table, "I do think we should have had quite a good chance with our knife, if it really is old—and finding it in Wichwood and everything—"

"What about sending in the penny that Mr. Murphy gave you ?" suggested Susan.

"I wouldn't dare!" said Bill. "Horrid Mr. Pilkington would be sure to see it and grab it just for spite. Oh *bother* that Selina—her and her friend in the British Museum!"

"And her friend in the B.B.C. And her friend who writes plays—" said Charlotte.

Susan said, "What about foisting her off on our friend who writes books ?"

"If only we could!" said Midge.

CHAPTER EIGHT

NO LUCK WITH RELATIONS

BUT THEIR friend who wrote books had not been inside the house ten minutes before they had all decided quite firmly that they wanted him for themselves and that he was much too nice to be foisted off on Selina. To start with, he arrived in a most magnificent American car which was about three miles long and broad in proportion, as Midge said. Susan and the Carmichaels were dumb with wonder, but Mr. Dean laughed in an embarrassed sort of way and said that he had had the car sent over by sea from South Africa, where most people went in for that kind of car because of the long straight roads and the vast distances; but that he was finding it more of a nuisance than anything else in England, it didn't seem to fit, somehow, and when he had driven it up from Southampton the day before he kept getting stuck in narrow little village streets and causing awful traffic jams because he couldn't get it round corners in one movement but had to back, usually into a flock of sheep or a cow or something. As soon as he could find a nice English car of suitable dimensions he would sell this one. And then seeing their disappointed faces he suggested that if they would like a drive in it first perhaps they could arrange it. This was very satisfactory; in fact Mr. Dean altogether was very satisfactory.

He was ancient, of course, about Aunt Lucy's age,
nearly forty, but he was jolly good fun and he told
them about his farm in the Orange Free State, and
climbs that he had done in the Drakensberg mountains, and adventures that he had had with lions
and other wild and savage animals although, as he
said in reply to Bill's question, he had never actually
shot a lion except with his ciné-camera. And he
told them how he had met Mr. and Mrs. Lyle,
Susan's parents, at a party in Johannesburg and how
the subject of Wichwood had come up because he
said he was going to visit it when he went to
England because his grandfather had come from
there and it would be nice to discover if any of his
relations still lived there, although he didn't think
they did. And so of course Susan's mother had told
him about Susan and the Carmichaels, and it had
been arranged that Mr. Dean should get in touch
with them—and here was the little parcel that he
had brought.

The little parcel contained lion-skin purses for the
girls, and for Bill, seeing that he wouldn't be interested in a purse, a native mask, a horrible looking
thing of black and white wood with fearful designs
painted on it and holes for the eyes and mouth.

Bill adored it. He held it up in front of his face
and went into the kitchen to frighten Mrs. Taylor,
and came prancing back to the hall where Mr. Dean
and the girls were still sitting. "Now I know what
I'll go to the fancy dress as! A witch-doctor!" he
cried. "Oh Mr. Dean, sir, d'you think you could
help me, tell me what to wear ?"

Mr. Dean said that of course he could, but he was

claimed by the grown-ups at that moment and the children saw him no more that evening. However, he left a note for Bill, which Aunt Lucy gave to him next morning. *Sorry I couldn't help with your costume to-night,* the note said, *but Mrs. Gascoigne has asked me for lunch on Saturday, so I'll come early and help you with it then. Can you collect:—coloured crepe paper, lots of bones, feathers, beads and, if possible, a lion-skin or leopard-skin? Yours, Gavin Dean.*

There was a stunned silence when Bill read this out. "Mrs. Gascoigne asked him for lunch!" exploded Midge, entirely forgetting Susan's foisting scheme. "Well, of all the cheek! He's our friend!"

"It was very kind of Mrs. Gascoigne," said Aunt Lucy primly. "He wants to explore Wichwood and find his relations—"

"Yes, but we were going to find his relations for him!" cried Susan. "We had it all arranged last night! We were going to the Vicar this morning to ask to see the parish records!"

"Oh well," said Aunt Lucy, and the children somehow had the feeling that she was not any more pleased than they were that Gavin Dean was going to the Gascoignes', "he's coming here first to help Bill with his costume—for coffee, at eleven or so."

"And I've got to collect all those things he said!" cried Bill. "Aunt Lucy, have you a lot of old bones for a witch-doctor's necklace?"

Aunt Lucy thought that any old bones that they might have had would be in the dustbin by now, but why didn't he go down the village and speak nicely to the butcher—a big marrow-bone, chopped up and boiled and the marrow removed would make a nice necklace for a witch-doctor, she should think—and the stock would do for soup, she added.

"And a lion's skin ?" asked Bill. "Where d'you think I'd find a lion's skin ?"

"Well, for goodness' sake!" said Aunt Lucy. "I don't know—"

Susan said, "Old Mrs. Thorne has a lion's skin, d'you think she would lend it to you ?"

"That's a brain-wave, Susie. D'you think I could ask her, Aunt Lucy ?" said Bill.

Aunt Lucy thought that he could, if he promised to take the greatest care of it.

Because there was not too much time and because Midge was too lazy anyway to walk all the way down the village to the vicarage and back to Mill-pond Cottages, they decided to separate; Charlotte and Bill to go to see the vicar and buy bones, Susan and Midge to go up to Mrs. Thorne.

Charlotte and Bill had more success with the bones than they had with the vicar; the butcher gave them a huge basket of bones of all shapes and sizes; but when they asked the vicar about the parish records he told them with much regret that the records had all been lost in the blitz of 1940. "And I don't suppose," Charlotte said, "that you remember people called Dean who used to live here —oh, about sixty years ago ?"

The vicar said that he didn't, but then he wouldn't, as he had only been in Wichwood himself for twenty years. "Old Mrs. Thorne's the one you want to see," he suggested. "Her father was vicar here about sixty years ago and she knew everybody—

Wichwood was a much smaller place in those days too—"

"Bother," said Bill, when they had thanked him and departed. "Susan and Midge could have asked when they were there—"

"Oh well," said Charlotte, "there's no hurry, really."

As a matter of fact, it did occur to Susan and Midge to ask Mrs. Thorne about Mr. Dean's relations, because she was pretty ancient and had, they knew, lived in Wichwood for simply donkeys' ages, but when they reached the little house and found Mrs. Thorne in tears, everything else went out of their heads.

"I'm just a silly old woman," Mrs. Thorne said, wiping her eyes and trying to smile. "And really I should be laughing and not crying because I've found a room—yes, a very nice woman who lives in Cox's Grove saw my notice in the toyshop window and has offered me a room. I went round to see it this morning and it is very nice and clean —small, of course, and rather cold in winter I'm afraid because it faces north, and of course it is furnished already so that I shan't be able to take any of my things, and one becomes so accustomed to one's own things round one, perhaps it's silly, but there it is—however, I must be thankful for small mercies—"

Midge and Susan didn't say anything. They thought that if they spoke they would howl like dogs at the sight of Mrs. Thorne glancing round her little sitting-room with the tears starting to her eyes again, and her old hands trembling as they screwed her handkerchief into a ball. "So," she went on at last, "I shall tell my landlord to go ahead with his plans for selling the house to Mr. Pilkington—there's no need now to wait until the ninth—"

"Oh Mrs. Thorne," Susan burst out, "*don't* tell him to-day! Wait until the ninth! Somebody might leave you a fortune next week! And how furious you would be if the house had been sold to horrid Mr. Pilkington!"

Mrs. Thorne laughed. And at least, Midge thought, there's something to be said for Susan's nonsense if it makes the poor dear old lady laugh. "Who would leave me a fortune ?" Mrs. Thorne said. "I'm afraid I haven't a relation left in the world!"

"Mrs. Thorne," said Susan earnestly, "did you ever hear that this house belonged to an old miser before it was let to you and that when he died his hoards of gold and money were never found ? And don't you think they might be still hidden in the house ?"

"Yes, I did hear that tale, Susan," said Mrs. Thorne, "and there was some truth in it—"

"Well then!" said Susan.

"But he wasn't as silly as some misers, Susan, because his hoards were safely in the post office savings bank!"

"Och, futer!" said Susan in disgust.

"A fairy-tale ending would be delightful," said Mrs. Thorne, "but I'm afraid it's not for me—and I shall be quite all right with Mrs. Nethersole, I'm sure."

"At least, Mrs. Thorne," Susan begged, "*please* don't tell your landlord yet! Not to-day, anyway—"

"The sooner I'm settled the better, Susan dear," said Mrs. Thorne, "but all right, to please you, I shan't say anything to him until Monday, anyway. And now I'm going to find you a glass of milk and I think there's still a slice of gingerbread in the tin—"

Over their milk and gingerbread the girls remembered what they had come for, and asked Mrs. Thorne about the lion's skin. She said that of course Bill could have the loan of it, in fact he might have it to keep, because Mrs. Nethersole might not like her to hang a lion's skin up on her wall, and Midge said well, perhaps they'd better wait and see about that because Mrs. Nethersole might be terribly nice and let her have all sorts of her own things—not tables and chairs and beds perhaps, but pictures and ornaments and certainly the lion's skin.

"Perhaps she will," said Mrs. Thorne. "And now I come to think of it, I have a box of ostrich feathers upstairs in the spare room cupboard, would a witch-doctor wear ostrich feathers, do you suppose?"

Midge said that she didn't know what was considered correct wear for witch-doctors, but that she was sure that their witch-doctor would absolutely adore ostrich feathers, so the kind old lady went upstairs to look them out.

Midge and Susan sat eating gingerbread and drinking milk in deep gloom. "I was going to be so clever and do something to help Mrs. Thorne!" said Susan at last. "Och, I should give up helping people and mind my own business! What good have I done Mrs. Thorne ?"

"Well, but Susie," said Midge, "what *could* you do ?"

"Och, I should have thought of something," said Susan. "What I *did* think," she added, "was that we might go and see this Mrs. Nethersole and persuade her to let Mrs. Thorne have some of her own things—"

Midge said cautiously, "Well, I don't know—perhaps we'd better keep out of that, in case we put our foot in it. Aunt Lucy may be able to fix something—better say nothing about it."

When Mrs. Thorne came back with the glorious ostrich feathers, Susan remembered to ask about Mr. Dean's relations, but Mrs. Thorne couldn't remember anyone called Dean in Wichwood, except a Miss Dean who had married Lord Oakfield who lived in that big house in Gallery Road. The girls didn't think that a Lady Oakfield could be any connection of their Mr. Dean, and they told Mrs. Thorne how nice he was.

"Could we bring him up to see you one day, Mrs. Thorne ?" said Susan. "Perhaps if you talk to him you might remember his relations, or people who knew them—"

Mrs. Thorne said that she would be delighted to see Mr. Dean, but that they had better bring him soon, because she would have to be thinking about her removal—and that set them all thinking again about that sad event, and in very low spirits Susan and Midge went home.

CHAPTER NINE

TREACHERY!

WHEN THEY reached home, the post had brought a long envelope for Midge.

"What on earth is this dreary-looking letter?" she said, slitting it open.

It was the manuscript of her story about the dragons and the small boys, and with it was a letter that said:—

Dear Miss Carmichael,

I have read your story, THE GREEDY DRAGON, and although I like it very much myself, I am afraid that it would not be at all suitable for "Listen with Mother", as I fear the children would all run from their loudspeakers shrieking with terror. Thank you very much for letting me see it—

"Goodness," said Midge, "all that boring afternoon when I sat writing simply wasted."

Susan said, "I wonder what happened to Gaby's stories. Shall we go and ask her?"

Midge would rather die, she said, than voluntarily seek out a ghastly Gascoigne.

"Och, but I'm dying to know," said Susan.

"We'll know soon enough. Unfortunately," said Midge.

Gabreille arrived just after elevenses. "Oh," she said, "Selina couldn't remember the time of the fancy-dress this afternoon— ?"

Midge told her. She was determined not to ask about Gabrielle's little stories, and at last Gabrielle was obliged to say, elaborately casual, "Oh by the way, did you hear from the B.B.C. ?"

"Yes," said Midge. "They thought my story would make the little perishers run shrieking from their loudspeakers—"

"Oh bad luck," said Gabrielle, and waited to be asked the fate of her stories. But nobody did, and Midge, with a malicious grin on her face, was just branching off on another subject when Gabrielle said hurriedly, "Mine were accepted. At least the drill is that they say they'll keep them and take copies, although this doesn't necessarily mean they'll be broadcast, but Selina's friend says that they never do keep them unless they mean to use them. But of course I shan't be paid until after the broadcast."

"How much," said Susan, and the words almost choked her, "will they pay you ?"

"How much ?" said Gabrielle, as if it didn't matter. "Oh—five guineas, I believe—each." And she went away.

"Five guineas!" said Susan through set teeth. "Just what we need to pay Mrs. Thorne's bill!"

"And to think, I sat up there in the orchard for a whole afternoon slaving away at that dragon," said Midge. "All for nothing."

"Och away, you were asleep half the time," said Susan. "But I really do grudge Gaby those five guineas."

"Ten guineas," Midge reminded her.

Susan and Charlotte had not been able to think of any original ideas for the fancy-dress fête. Aunt Lucy had eventually suggested that Charlotte might wear her grandmother's wedding-dress—she was just about the right height for it now if she wasn't too hefty—and Aunt Lucy had brought it down from its box upstairs and laid it on Charlotte's bed, smelling strongly of moth-balls. Aunt Lucy helped her into it. "Can you breathe?" she said anxiously, doing up the hooks.

"Well, I can," said Charlotte, "only I'll die of heat—!" For the dress, of very heavy satin going yellow with age, had a tight waist, heavily boned, long tight sleeves and a high neck.

Mrs. Taylor poked her head round the door. "Oh Charlotte, ducks, you look lovely," she said. "Doesn't she, Mum? Quite a picture—" Midge and Susan agreed with her fervently, and buoyed up by this praise, Charlotte decided that she could endure the heat and discomfort.

"I'll make you a little posy of flowers," said Aunt Lucy, "with a paper doily for a frill if only I can find a paper doily—we did have some, somewhere— And what can you wear on your head?"

Bill, who had looked in to inquire if Gavin had arrived yet, said in a brotherly sort of way, a long, very thick veil, but you could see that he too was impressed by Charlotte's looks.

Aunt Lucy said vaguely, "A veil, of course! What about that old lace curtain that lay about in the kitchen drawer for ages? Well, come on, Charlotte, come and help me to find something that will do as a veil—I'll fix up a little cap or something for you."

Susan had decided to go as Billy Bunter in Bill's school cap and blazer and a lot of Aunt Lucy's cushions. "I really will die of heat," she complained. "This is much worse than Charlotte's tight satin."

"We've all chosen very stupidly for a hot day," Midge agreed, "except Bill. He should be all right in nothing but paper streamers and a lion's skin round his chest."

Gavin Dean came and gave his expert advice on correct wear for witch-doctors—which in this case was a sort of skirt made of strips of coloured paper, the lion's skin fastened over one shoulder, beads and bones round the neck and ostrich feathers surmounting the terrible mask.

"You really do look absolutely frightening," said Midge, "even with white, if not very clean, skin showing—"

There was a slight argument as to how Bill was going to blacken himself. He wanted to use black boot polish and Aunt Lucy was afraid that that would never come off.

"Soot then—" said Bill.

Aunt Lucy shuddered.

Gavin Dean, who had been helping Susan to pad herself with cushions, now said that he had brought some sticks of black grease-paint with him, because he had vivid memories of doing himself up once with boot polish and he hadn't been able to get it off for what seemed in retrospect like months, but was probably only weeks.

"I *do* wish that you weren't going off to the silly

old Gascoignes, for lunch," grumbled Bill, "when you could have been such a help to us. What did *they* want to ask you for?"

"Bill!" said Aunt Lucy.

"Well apparently," said Gavin Dean apologetically, "I'm to meet a celebrated artist called Sam Pilkington, of whom, of course, I had already heard —as we're not the absolute barbarians in South Africa that some people think. I'm to meet him because he knows a lot about old Wichwood and he might, Mrs. Gascoigne thinks, also know about my long-lost relations."

"I'm sure that horrid Mr. Pilkington couldn't *poss*ibly know anything about anybody's relations," muttered Midge, but quietly, so that Aunt Lucy shouldn't hear.

And Susan said, "Oh, Mr. Dean, we did ask a very great friend of ours who is very old and knows a lot more about old Wichwood than Mr. Pilkington and she didn't remember any Deans in Wichwood except one who married a lord or somebody—"

"But my grandfather's name wasn't Dean," said Gavin Dean. "It was my mother's father who came from Wichwood and his name was Martin, James Martin."

"Oh well," said Susan, "that's *different*. Cheer up, Mr. Dean, we'll ask our friend again and I expect she'll know your grandfather James Martin terribly well—"

"Much better than horrid Mr. Pilkington, anyway," muttered Midge.

Gavin Dean grinned at the anti-Pilkington party. "Will you all have supper with me after this beanfeast this afternoon?" he said. Susan and the Carmichaels looked all eagerness. "Is there some place here where we can go?"

"Well, there's the White Hart," said Charlotte, "but I don't know if Aunt Lucy would be very keen on our going there because it's really a pub, although an awfully nice one—"

"Oh well," said Gavin Dean, "we can go up to town, to the Ritz or some place like that."

"The Ritz!" they said, big-eyed, and the female members of the family thought nervously that their clothes would hardly come up to Ritz standards.

"That's settled then," said Gavin Dean. "And now I suppose I'd better go. But first you must throw your bones, Bill—"

"Throw my bones?" exclaimed Bill, with a vision of his frame, which was fairly bony, being tossed about from hand to hand.

"These bones," said Gavin, pointing to Bill's collection of marrow bones and knuckle-bones, "you must throw these to see what the afternoon has in store for us—" and he picked up the bones in his hands, shook them and threw them on the floor. "Ah!" he said in a very sinister voice, "I predict treachery and double-dealing—"

Susan and the Carmichaels shivered delightedly. "Can you really foretell the future, Mr. Dean?" said Susan.

Gavin Dean laughed. "No, of course I can't. But witch-doctors are supposed to be able to tell the future with their bones—they say that during the war the witch-doctors who went with the African troops used to throw their bones to find out where the enemy were. You must do some bone-throwing, Bill, to add a little local colour." And with that Gavin Dean said good-bye to them and went off to the Gascoignes, saying he hoped that they would all win prizes . . .

Susan and the Carmichaels made an extraordinary picture as they stumped up Tollgate Road that afternoon to Mrs. Mountford-Jones's house at the corner opposite the old mill pond. They had tried very hard to persuade Dr. Carmichael to give them a lift, but in the end he had had to hurry out to a case and the family weren't ready; which made it all the more galling when Midge saw from a side window, as she was stuffing herself with straw, their own father ushering the ghastly Gascoignes and their own Mr. Dean into their own car and whisking them up Tollgate Road. It was a heavy, close, thundery day and everybody except Bill was in a state of extreme discomfort. They all complained bitterly as they crawled along, suiting their pace to that of the scarecrow.

"Och well," said Susan, "you can't blame Uncle Charles for giving the Gascoignes a lift and not us, when we weren't ready."

"I'm not blaming Daddy," said Midge, "I'm only blaming the ghastly Gascoignes. I suppose you all realise that *absolutely* everything has gone wrong since these Gascoignes came into our lives?"

Susan, overcome with heat, the weight of her cushion padding and emotion, said, "Och, I *know*, Midge, and it's all my fault! I said I'd do something about these Gascoignes—"

"Well, as you know, Susie darling, I thought it was a great mistake starting you off on those jobs at all," said Charlotte, "but *hon*estly I don't see how we can blame you for the turn events have taken."

"The fact of the matter is," said Midge, thinking of her first rejected manuscript, "that everything we can do, they can do better—"

They turned in at the gate of The Willows, and a gay sight met their eyes. Crowds milled round the laden stalls and gathered round the side-shows; small children were having pony rides on two Shetland ponies; on the lawns which stretched down to the willow-fringed pool, weird and wonderful figures were assembling.

"Oh blow and bother!" exclaimed Midge. "There's another scarecrow!"

Sure enough, in the middle of the lawn, immovable, arms stiffly pointed, bottle-straw legs astraddle, stood a scarecrow.   -

"But," said Susan doubtfully, "surely that's a real scarecrow ?"

"What would Mrs. Mountford-Jones be doing with a scarecrow in the middle of her lawn ?" said Charlotte. "It's someone in fancy dress."

"Well it's terribly good, that's all I can say," said Susan. "Let's go and have a closer look."

Susan, Charlotte and Bill hurried off across the lawn, leaving their own scarecrow far behind, and joined the small crowd that was circling round the scarecrow, making admiring remarks.

"Oh hallo," said the scarecrow, "you *are* late. I thought you weren't coming."

"*Gabrielle!*" said Charlotte.

For a second Susan was speechless. She could hardly believe her ears—but that was Gabrielle's voice all right; or her eyes—but that was Gabrielle's face, peering out from between the straw with which she had half-covered her face. "Well!" she burst out at last. "You mean beast! You *knew* Midge was coming as a scarecrow! We told you!"

"Did you ?" said Gabrielle carelessly. "*I* don't remember—"

Mrs. Gascoigne, looking cool and exquisite in a grey dress with a pattern of tiny white shells all over it, came up. "Oh hallo, you darling Carmichaels, how *won*derful you all look! Really funny, Susan, just the right build for Billy Bunter! Isn't my Gabrielle *the* perfect scarecrow ? I keep getting quite a turn when I catch sight of her out of the corner of my eye—I mean, she just *is* a scarecrow—oh, *no*, oh how too maddening! Gabrielle darling, look, there's another scarecrow—!"

"Yes," said Susan furiously, "it's Midge!"

"Oh," said Selina coldly. "Rather a pity to copy Gabrielle, don't you think ? Gabrielle has been talking about going as a scarecrow for days—"

Charlotte and Bill stood in sullen silence. Susan was now an alarming sort of puce colour with rage. "C-c-c-copy Gabrielle!" she stuttered. "The foot's on the other boot! Gabrielle—"

"Oh, there's our nice Gavin looking *rather* lost, poor sweet!" Selina interrupted. "I must run and look after him!" She bent her elegant head towards Charlotte and whispered, "Do persuade your sister to go home. Such a disappointment for my little Gabrielle—!"

Without answering, Charlotte turned and marched off in the direction of Midge, lumbering towards them on her straw legs. Bill and Susan, with furious glares at Gabrielle who smiled sweetly at them, followed her.

When they came up to Midge, Charlotte cried, "Who d'you think the scarecrow is ?"

"Gabrielle, I suppose. I saw That Woman with you," said Midge, and sighed. "Oh well, a lot of energy wasted— Do come into a corner with me and help to get all these things off—"

"You're not going to take them off!" cried Susan.

"You're not just calmly going to give in!" cried Charlotte. "That's what That Woman wants you to do! She told me to persuade you to go home!"

"Let's go and tear the things off Gabrielle!" cried Bill.

"Oh goodness," said Midge in a tired voice, "we can't start a brawl in Mrs. Mountford-Jones's garden!"

"Well, at least you can also enter for the parade and spoil her chances," said Susan vindictively.

"Frankly," said Midge, taking off her battered old hat and pulling straw out of her disreputable jacket, "I couldn't be bothered." She sat down on the grass and Bill pulled the bottle-straws off her legs. "Think how cool I shall be while you're all sweating round in the parade," she said. "Only, I don't suppose any of you have a comb, by any chance ? I'd better find Aunt Lucy and borrow one from her—"

She left her scarecrow clothes in a heap to be collected later, and walked across the lawn with the

others. The competitors were beginning to gather
for the fancy dress parade, and the scarecrow was
stiff and immovable in the middle of the lawn.
Midge went up to her. "What a mean beast you
are, Gabrielle," she said in her lazy drawl and
walked away.

CHAPTER TEN

INTERESTING AND CURIOUS OBJECTS

As SUSAN said afterwards—over and over again—
she nearly burst a blood-vessel when Gabrielle won
first prize. That Charlotte and Bill won prizes too
was some consolation, but when Susan and Midge
rushed up to them after the competition was over,
they were much chagrined to find that Bill's prize
was a very handsome knife with at least six blades
and a thing for taking stones out of horses' hoofs,
and that Charlotte's was a box of chocolates.

"No money!" said Susan. "Och, it's awful to be
pot-hunting like this," she added apologetically;
"and it's a lovely knife, Bill, and normally there's
nothing I'd like Charlotte to win better than
chocolates, but—och, well, we need the money so
badly! And there's that mean sneak got two pounds
that Midge should have had—"

"Let's go and see the Exhibition of Interesting and
Curious objects," said Midge soothingly.

Susan removed Aunt Lucy's cushions amid sighs
of relief, and left them with Midge's scarecrow
things. Home-made sign-posts led them to the
drawing-room of the house where the interesting
and curious objects were laid out. At the door they
met Peregrine, who was dressed, appropriately
enough, as a small red devil.

"You've missed the fancy dress parade, Pea-green,"
said Midge.

"Oh, how provoking," said Peregrine, but not with much conviction.

"Gabrielle won first prize," said Susan sourly, "as a scarecrow. She stole the idea from Midge."

Peregrine said nothing, only made a face and slipping between Susan and Midge sped off across the grass where most of the spectators were steaming towards the roped-off piece of lawn labelled TEAS 1/6.

"Oh good," said Midge as they went into the exhibition, "no one here."

The exhibits, neatly labelled, were laid out on a long table, and there was a notice asking people to vote on the most interesting exhibit, the owner of which would be awarded a prize.

"I wish the owners' names were given," said Midge, "so that we could be sure not to vote for anything exhibited by the ghastly Gascoignes—"

Susan was puzzling over an exhibit and its label. "Look at this, Midge," she said. "Exhibit 3. The label says, *Piece of Thorn-tree to which William Wallace tied his horse when visiting friends in 1297. Actual tree blown down in 1870*—now that's very interesting, don't you think ? But the exhibit doesn't look at all like a bit of an old tree to me, it looks just like a bird's egg—"

Midge looked at the label and at the exhibit. "It *is* a bird's egg," she said.

"And look at this!" Susan moved on to another curiosity. "The ticket says *Pearl-handled knife and fork used by Florence Nightingale*. Does that look like a pearl-handled knife and fork to you ?"

Midge examined the exhibit and said that it looked like a set of doll's house furniture to her.

"And—oh look at this one, how sweet!" cried Susan. "It's the tiniest wee spinning-wheel inside a cherry-stone or a nut or something like that!"

"The card says, *Handkerchief presented to all school children in Glasgow on the death of Queen Victoria*," said Midge.

"Well," said Susan, looking perplexedly about her, "I think this is a jolly queer exhibition."

Light seemed to dawn on Midge all of a sudden. "I don't think that it's a queer exhibition so much," she said slowly, "as that it has had a visit from Pea-green—"

"Pea-green?" said Susan impatiently. "What's Pea-green got to do with it?"

Midge waved languidly at the table. "Don't you recognise the hand of Pea-green in all this?" she murmured.

"The Hand of Pea-green?" said Susan stupidly, glancing at the exhibits as if expecting to see Pea-green's dismembered hand among them. "Oh, you mean the *hand* of *Pea-green* did all this? Oh Midge, he never would!"

"Well, it seems to me just the kind of happy little thought that Pea-green would have," said Midge.

"Oh Midge! Oh well, we must change them all back again before anyone comes!" cried Susan in her helpful way," and she grabbed an object that looked like a brass cannon-ball. "First of all this cricket-ball or whatever it is—" But Susan must have been excited or something and her hands must have been slippery because it slid through her fingers and went coursing down the length of the table, bowling over exhibits right and left before falling to the ground with a dull thud. It rolled across the floor and knocked over a small wine-table which in turn knocked over an old-fashioned pedestal on which stood a vase of flowers. The vase crashed over but fortunately—in a way—fell on to a sofa which had been pushed back against a wall.

"Susan, *really*—" began Midge.

"Well, honestly," said Susan, snatching at the vase and stuffing the flowers back into it in a very flustered way," sending cannon-balls to exhibitions! Not the thing at all—oh gosh, Midge, *look* at the sofa, what on earth am I to do about that ?"

The sofa might have saved the vase from smashing into small pieces, but at its own expense; it had received all the water from the vase and a huge damp stain was spreading along the pale green brocade.

"Well, you could sit on it," said Midge gravely. "That would hide most of it."

"Och, it doesn't!" cried Susan, trying it. "It only hides a wee bit!"

"Lie down then," said Midge.

"What will anybody think if they come in and find me lying full-length on the sofa ?" asked Susan.

"I can't imagine," said Midge. "But what'll they think if they see that stain ?"

"Och yes, that's true!" said Susan and lay back.

Midge righted the small wine-table, picked up the cannon-ball and wandered round the big table, looking for a card which might describe what it was. She saw Florence Nightingale's knife and fork and put their card with them. "I don't suppose it occurred to your monumental brain," she said, "that it would be easier to move the cards?"

"So it would," said Susan, wriggling a little uncomfortably on her sofa, for the damp was beginning to seep through the trousers belonging to Bill that she was still wearing.

Midge glanced across the table at her. "Is your idea to loll there while I do all the work?" she inquired mildly.

"No, no, of course not," said Susan guiltily and jumped to her feet. She began frenziedly moving tickets.

Suddenly there was a sound of approaching footsteps on the flagged terrace outside the french windows. "Somebody coming!" gasped Susan and flung herself back on the sofa.

It was unfortunate that it was Mrs. Mountford-Jones who came into the room at that moment. Mrs. Mountford-Jones was normally a perfectly pleasant woman and the Carmichaels liked her quite well; but this fête had been on her mind a bit—first of all if the weather would hold up and then if anybody would come if it did, and then about five hundred more people than her wildest dreams turned up and the next worry was if there would be enough food. And then that extraordinary business on the tea lawn, with the sugar inexplicably turned into salt—she had put the sugar into the basins herself that morning and it certainly wasn't salt then—and now she comes up to the house to see how things are going there, and catches sight through the window of these two girls behaving very oddly indeed—one reclining full-length on her newly covered sofa cushions and the other fiddling with the cards. If this was some kind of a joke, she thought, the time to nip it in the bud was *now*—and wild accusations sprang to her lips.

What terrifying person! Susan thought. She went quite pale and shrank back against the wet cushions. Midge listened in silence and at the first opportunity she interrupted calmly, "Mrs. Mountford-Jones, we're not muddling up the exhibition, *honestly*, we're trying to un-muddle it. We came in to have a look and found it like this—"

"Now how could that have happened ?—And the salt instead of sugar—Midge, I *do* apologise, but I—" she spoke in disjointed snatches and began rushing round the table distractedly moving exhibits, like Susan had done, only not with such disastrous results, until Midge managed to hint tactfully that she found it easier to move the cards. "Well, of course it is—silly of me—" said poor Mrs. Mountford-Jones, and in her confusion glanced across at Susan. "Can't *you* help ?"

"I—I—I—I" Susan said—if you could call it speaking.

"Are you ill ?" Mrs. Mountford-Jones said a little sharply. This awkward girl with an infectious disease would be just about the last straw.

"Susan's a little bit dizzy," Midge put in. And goodness knows, she thought, *that's* the truth—!

"She *is* very pale," said Mrs. Mountford-Jones, looking at Susan rather irritably and wishing that she wouldn't *spread* herself so. "Perhaps *sal volatile*—"

"Oh, *no* thank you, Mrs. Mountford-Jones," said Susan. She didn't know who Sal Volatile was and she didn't want to find out. "I'll be quite all right —just the sun—"

Midge remembered that the sun hadn't shone all day and said quickly, "Hadn't we better finish these cards, Mrs. Mountford-Jones— ?"

Mrs. Mountford-Jones hurriedly went on re-arranging, and soon all was in order again. Some people began to trickle in; Mrs. Mountford-Jones went off to bustle round some other section of the fête; Midge went over to Susan. "I think we ought to vote and then go," she said. "I'm getting slightly bored with this exhibition."

"How can I go ?" asked Susan. "I daren't get up."

"Well, you can't stay here for the rest of your life," said Midge. "Mrs. Mountford-Jones would hate it."

Susan giggled. "Not as much as I would," she said. "All right, then, let's vote, and when everybody is looking at the exhibits I'll try to slip out. I'm going to vote for that wee spinning-wheel. Go and see what its number is for me, will you ?"

Midge said that she would and thought that she herself would vote for the grain of rice inscribed with a hundred and fifty letters and numbers, which was exhibited under a magnifying glass.

"Och away," said Susan, "I think that's a silly exhibit. Who wants to write a hundred and fifty letters and figures on a grain of rice ? Besides, how d'you know there *are* a hundred and fifty letters and figures on it ?"

"Well, I'm not going to sit on that damp sofa while you count them, anyway," murmured Midge.

"But I'm still going to vote for it—it's number five, and your spinning-wheel in a cherry-stone is number thirty-three—"

Midge put their votes in the box provided for the purpose, and acted as cover for Susan while she took a hasty look at the sofa and sidled through the french windows. "I thought the stain was drying off nicely," Susan said hopefully as they hurried away from the house across the lawn towards the side-shows. "Didn't you?"

"Frankly, no," said Midge. "And all I hope is that we never meet Mrs. Mountford-Jones again in the whole of our lives—"

They saw Charlotte, looking absolutely beautiful, as Susan said, in her wedding satin, talking to a strange young man. He was tall and dark and very good-looking, and when Charlotte saw them, she blushed and looked uncomfortable and half-turned her back on them and did not acknowledge them.

"What's the matter with Charlotte?" asked Susan, gaping.

Midge didn't know. "To think," she said melodramatically, "that my only sister is ashamed to speak to me!"

Susan giggled. "Well, when you look at us it's perhaps not surprising," she said humbly. "I'm all wet from lying on that sofa and you've still got straw in your hair."

They drifted to the "Fish-pond", where Peregrine was standing with a toy fishing-rod in his hand and an evil sort of leer on his face, surrounded by piles of handsome winnings. The pretty girls who were assisting at the Fish-pond had hunted looks on their faces.

The "Fish-pond" consisted of little tin fish that were hooked with little fishing-rods, and according as the "catch" consisted of a sprat or a sole or a whale, a prize was received. A sprat or a dab ranked a plastic egg-cup or a sample packet of custard; a sole or a cod or a trout won a pocket-comb or a bar of toffee, but a whale won a really handsome prize, a box of chocolates or a "crystal" dish. "Oh, hallo," said Peregrine, "have you come to watch me fish? I'm a very good fisher—" He nodded condescendingly and then leant over the rim of the Fish-pond angling for his tin fish. "They want me to go and try the Wheel of Fortune, but I might not win at the Wheel of Fortune—Ah!" he said nonchalantly, "Another whale, I think—!"

The pretty assistants muttered among themselves. Then one handed Peregrine a handsome china teapot, and another said, "How much money have you left?"

Peregrine felt in his pocket and looked chagrined. "I haven't any left," he said. "But," he said, brightening, "I expect Selina will give me some more when she hears how good I am at fishing—" He began to gather up his prizes while the assistants looked at him with hatred. Susan, who couldn't resist giving a helping hand, even to Pea-green, piled the boxes into his outstretched arms, tucked a gorgeous crystal vase under one arm and the teapot under the other. Peregrine staggered off.

Midge and Susan looked longingly at the Fish-pond. Aunt Lucy had given them each some money to spend at the fête, but with Miss Thorne's bill looming over them they could scarcely bear to part with it.

"Yet we ought to spend it at the fête because that's what Aunt Lucy gave it to us for," said Susan.

"Yes, but not on the Fish-pond," sighed Midge regretfully, "because I can tell you here and now that we shouldn't catch a whale—and a shilling a shot is rather expensive if we only get a sample tube of toothpaste or something like that out of it. Let's go to the stalls and see if we can buy something useful for Aunt Lucy or Daddy."

On their way to the fancy-work stall they again passed Charlotte, who was still talking to the strange young man. This time she deliberately cut them dead.

"What *is* the matter with us ?" said Susan, feeling quite put out. Such behaviour was totally unlike Charlotte.

"You mean, more than usual ?" said Midge.

"Well, why doesn't she want to know us ?"

"I don't think it's us," said Midge, "I think it's Charlotte. She's got a guilty conscience about something. She always goes frightfully peculiar when she's feeling guilty—"

They had the good luck to find some of Aunt Lucy's toffee at the sweet stall and they spent two shillings on that. That was for themselves; at the second-hand book stall they bought a very exciting looking thriller for Uncle Charles for a shilling, and for another shilling a ghastly tome about Ur of the Chaldees which they hoped was on archæology for Charlotte. Unfortunately it turned out to be in German, but Susan said that was nothing to a

S.R.I.   E

keen archæologist. For Bill they bought a very
old but rather nice copy of a book called *The Story
of the Treasure Seekers*, and this they got for threepence. It was old-fashioned and they had never
heard of the author who was somebody called E.
Nesbit, but it was obviously a children's book and
just right, they thought, for Bill with his own
fondness for treasure seeking. They went on to the
arts and crafts stall and found there a lovely little
fat blue and white striped vase. It had a chip in it
and so had been marked down to five shillings. This
was perfect for Aunt Lucy, they felt, and the chip
would *never* be seen. The lady at the stall beamed
at them as she took their money "You've got a
bargain," she said. "It's one of Mrs. Gascoigne's—
look!" She turned the pot upside down and showed
them the signature, *Selina*.

Midge took the pot much as she would have taken
a viper in her hand. The girls thanked the lady
stall-holder and turned away, their heads close
together and bent over the pot.

"Let's dash it to the ground, now, this minute!"
said Midge.

"And waste five shillings!" exclaimed Susan, her
Scottish blood in revolt. "Besides, Midge," she
added in honesty, "we liked it before we knew That
Woman made it."

Midge said, "Mm," in a doubtful sort of way.

Their purchases made, they were now left with
ninepence, which would not even buy them one
tea, far less two. Susan suggested that they should
go down to the tea-lawn and see if any of the teas
were being marked down in price.

"You're an optimist," said Midge.

"I'd eat the crumbs that fall from the rich man's table, *willingly*," said Susan, "I'm starving. Lunch, you must admit, with everybody late and trying to get dressed, was a bit sketchy—"

"Well, *there* you are," said a voice, and Gavin Dean stood before them. "I was just looking for someone to have tea with, but your aunt was busy and Bill has had three teas already, although he very kindly said he'd come in with me again to keep me company, and Charlotte is still deep in converse with Adrian—"

"With who?" asked Midge, hoping that she hadn't heard properly, but knowing in her bones that she had.

"With Adrian Gascoigne," said Mr. Dean calmly. "He arrived home last night, I met him at lunch."

"Treachery!" muttered Susan through her teeth to Midge.

"No wonder she looked guilty!" Midge muttered back.

"Well," said Gavin, who couldn't make head or tail of this muttering, "what about tea?"

"Oh, we'd love it," said Susan fervently.

"Wouldn't you rather have tea with—with Peregrine?" asked Midge, catching sight of a gleam of red out of the corner of her eye. After all, if Charlotte had deserted to the other camp, what more likely than that their nice Mr. Dean would go over too, if he wasn't already there?

"Frankly," said Mr. Dean, "no."

Well that was some comfort, and they settled themselves at a very nice table from which they could command an excellent view of all that was going on. Midge and Susan regretted this a few minutes later when Charlotte sat down at a near-by table with the hated Gascoigne.

"I hope the sight of them doesn't put me off my food," said Susan to Midge as Mr. Dean ordered tea.

"I hope *her* food chokes her," said Midge.

"It won't," said Susan sadly. "There's no justice in this world."

"I hope he's madly boring about his silly old digs and she doesn't understand a word he says," said Midge.

"I hope he didn't dig up a single broken old pot," said Susan.

"I hope he fell in all the holes," said Midge.

Mr. Dean said mildly, "You sound like a couple of old witches uttering spells—what has poor Adrian done to deserve this?"

Susan blushed furiously and Midge said uncomfortably, "Oh sorry, Mr. Dean, we shouldn't have been talking like this in front of you. After all, perhaps they're friends of yours—"

"You've eaten their salt," said Susan solemnly.

"Mm," Mr. Dean agreed. "I nearly ate their frogs as well. Peregrine put a frog in my soup and everybody thought it was funny, except me."

This cheered Midge and Susan up enormously. "*We* think Pea-green is quite boringly unfunny," Midge said happily, "but I must say that everybody else simply shrieks with laughter at his antics."

Susan said, wide-eyed and solemn, "Mr. Dean, you remember you threw the bones and predicted treachery this morning? Well, perhaps you'll be interested to know it happened! Twice! First Gabrielle, then—" she stopped. "Och well, we don't want to bore you with all that, but I thought you'd like to know that your predictions came true and you must be an awfully good bone-thrower."

Gavin Dean modestly disclaimed any skill in throwing the bones, and they chatted of this and that until the girls were at bursting-point and sat back with happy sighs. Gavin idly picked up their books. "What have you been buying?" he asked. "Oh, not *The Story of the Treasure Seekers*!" and he eagerly began to turn the pages.

"Why?" said Susan anxiously. "Is it no good?"

"Do you *know* this book?" asked Midge.

"Know it?" exclaimed Gavin. "But of course I do! It's by E. Nesbit."

"Yes," said Midge. "We'd never heard of E. Nesbit."

"Never heard of E. Nesbit! Is it possible!" said Gavin. "She was my favourite author when I was a child. Her books are classics."

"Really?" said Midge. "Oh well, that's quite good then, and we only paid threepence for it."

"We thought it would do for Bill," Susan explained. "He has been very keen himself about treasure-hunting lately. And s'matter of fact," she went on, trying not to sound too proud, "he and I did find a treasure, sort of, but of course That Woman—I mean—" she stopped in confusion, but Gavin obviously wasn't listening. He was examining *The Story of the Treasure Seekers* with great care.

"D'you know," he said slowly, "I think that this might be a first edition! Published in 1904."

Midge and Susan knew about first editions; they knew that some grown-ups thought a lot of first editions, thought that old—and in some cases dirty —first editions were better than nice new editions of exactly the same book. They knew that some people paid a lot of money for them—"D'you mean," Midge said slowly, "that it might be valuable ?"

"Well, I don't know," said Mr. Dean. "But I myself would willingly give .five or six pounds for it!"

Magic words! Five or six pounds! Enough to pay Mrs. Thorne's bill and perhaps even enough over to buy Bill a decent copy of *The Story of the Treasure Seekers*! Susan could hardly keep herself from shouting "Done!" and holding out her hand for the money.

"But perhaps," Mr. Dean said, glancing up at the silent girls, "perhaps you wouldn't want to part with it— ?"

"Oh goodness, *we* don't mind!" cried Susan, terrified that Mr. Dean would change his mind. "Do we, Midge ?"

"We'd love you to have it, Mr. Dean," said Midge earnestly, "wouldn't we, Susan ?"

"Well, that's very nice of you," said Mr. Dean. "And of course I'd find out if five or six pounds were the proper value—I should hate to cheat you—"

"Oh, don't bother!" cried Susan. "Five pounds would suit us nicely."

"But Mr. Dean," said Midge, suffering a little conscience-trouble because obviously Mr. Dean was quite carried away by finding this book that he had liked when he was a child, and it would be dreadful if he went back to his hotel and repented of his offer, "Mr. Dean, oughtn't you to think it over? I mean, five pounds is a lot of money!"

"Here's another thing!" exclaimed Susan, also having a slight attack of conscience. "What about the person who sent it to the fête?" A vision of another Mrs. Thorne, desperately needing money, floated before her unwilling eyes. "Oughtn't we to find out who sent it and tell them that it's valuable?"

"Well," said Midge reasonably enough, "obviously they didn't want it, or they wouldn't have sent it to the sale. But you could, I suppose, ask Mrs. Mountford-Jones who sent it."

"Me ask Mrs. Mountford-Jones!" cried Susan. "I'd rather die!" Mrs. Mountford-Jones, she thought, must have seen the mess her sofa was in by this time.

"We'll ask Aunt Lucy," said Midge. "She'll know what to do—"

The fête was almost over. At night there would be square-dancing under fairy lights strung all over the garden, but now the stalls were almost cleared and people were beginning to go home. Over the loud-speaker a voice announced the winner of the most popular exhibit in the "Home Curiosities". It was number five, the grain of rice inscribed with a hundred and fifty letters and—"As we might have guessed," muttered Midge—the owner was Peregrine Gascoigne.

"Who cares?" Susan muttered back. "The Gascoignes haven't an E. Nesbit first edition up their sleeves!"

CHAPTER ELEVEN

LION'S SKIN

THE CARMICHAELS and Susan and Gavin Dean straggled home down Tollgate Road. Charlotte, not looking at anyone and trying not to sound defiant, asked Aunt Lucy if it would be all right if she changed and went back to the dancing with Adrian Gascoigne. Aunt Lucy, delighted that at last one of her family seemed anxious to be friendly with those clever, interesting, original and amusing people next door, gave willing consent.

"Traitor!" muttered Susan.

"Snake in the grass!" hissed Midge.

"If he's anything like Pea-green," said Bill, "you're in for some fun. I expect he'll put worms down your back or—"

"He's not a bit like Pea-green!" cried Charlotte. "He has been telling me about this dig in Syria—*fasc*inating!" she said with dignity. "Besides, he can't help it if his family are all stinkers."

"No," said Bill, "that's true enough. But just be careful, that's all—"

"What's the matter with his mouth?" said Midge.

"There's nothing the matter with his mouth," said Charlotte defensively.

"Oh well, you should know, I suppose, considering that you were talking to him all afternoon," said Midge, "but I must say I thought there was something the matter with his mouth, didn't you, Susie?"

"Well," said Susan in a considering voice, "would you say there was something the *matter* with it? I thought he just had a hot potato in it—left over from lunch, I thought—"

"Goodness, I thought there was something wrong with his mouth or his teeth or something," said Midge.

"This was how he talked," said Bill, "like this—"

Susan and Midge and Bill all began to speak with hot potatoes in their mouths. Charlotte, purple with rage, flounced on ahead; and had her own revenge by bagging the top bathroom and staying in it for a very long time.

At Aunt Lucy's instigation, the venue for that evening's supper-party had been changed from the Ritz to something a little less grand in Soho; in fact Aunt Lucy wanted them all to stay at home and eat scrambled eggs and save Gavin's money. But Gavin said no, because if they stayed at home he would have to offer to wash the dishes, and if there was one thing that most South Africans didn't like about England it was washing dishes. Aunt Lucy said that in that case she thought that they ought to hurry or they would be too late to go anywhere, and Midge, who had collapsed on to her back on a chair and was tootling mournfully on her recorder, said that they couldn't hurry because Charlotte had bagged the bathroom, the mean pig, just like an associate of Gascoignes. Aunt Lucy, though inclined for a moment to flare up, kept calm by a great effort and said that they could use the downstairs bathroom.

This was exactly what Midge had been angling for, because the downstairs bathroom was much nicer than the old nursery one, which only had a painted bath and usually most of the paint was coming off it on to you in lumps except when it was newly painted and then you stuck to it. And also there were the bath salts which someone had given Aunt Lucy last Christmas and which she always forgot to use. Midge and Susan went off quite happily.

Gavin Dean offered to help the witch doctor out of his tribal dress, which offer Bill gratefully accepted. "It's always much more fun getting into fancy dress than getting out of it," he said.

Gavin Dean agreed. He carefully unpinned the lion's skin and smoothed it affectionately with his hand. "Lovely skin," he said, and folding it over he went to lay it on the bed. Then he stopped and stared at it. At the sudden silence Bill glanced up.

"What is it ?" said Bill.

"Look at this!" Gavin said, and pointed out some very neat, small writing on the back of the skin. "Look what it says— *James Martin shot this lion in Bechuanaland in 1884*!"

"Goodness," said Bill, "I never noticed that. I expect Mrs. Thorne wrote it—"

"Yes, but the funny thing is," said Gavin, "that my grandfather's name was James Martin!"

Bill gaped at him for a minute and then started dancing up and down as if he were witch-doctoring again. "But this is wonderful!" he shouted. "This lion may have been shot by your very own grandfather!"

"But in that case where did this Mrs. Thorne get it ?" said Gavin Dean.

"*I* don't know," cried Bill. "Perhaps this grandfather of yours sent it to her! Perhaps she knew your grandfather—!" He rushed to the door of his room and yelled, "Midge! *Susan*!"

Susan stuck her head over the top floor banisters and yelled back, "What is it ? Midge is in the bathroom—"

Bill leant his head back and looked up at Susan. "Susie!" he shouted. "We've found a clue to Mr. Dean's relations! Come down!"

Susan, clean and changed into her best dress, came charging downstairs. Bill was minutely examining the lion's skin in case there was any more writing that they had missed.

"Is that the clue ?" said Susan, stupefied.

"Yes, look," said Bill and pointed to the inscription. "It says, *James Martin shot this lion in Bechuanaland in 1884* and his—" he jerked his head at Mr. Dean, "I mean, Mr. Dean's grandfather's name was James Martin, so perhaps it's the same James Martin and Mrs. Thorne may be able to tell us something about him! I don't suppose Mrs. Thorne said where this lion's skin came from ?"

Midge, pink from too hot a bath, came out of the bathroom in her dressing-gown. She eagerly entered into the discussion, but she didn't remember Mrs. Thorne ever mentioning where she had got the lion's skin.

"The obvious thing to do," said Susan, "is go up there now and find out."

"What, now?" said Midge. "Walk all the way up to Millpond Cottages?"

"What, now?" said Mr. Dean. "What about our dinner?"

"Well, shall Bill and I go alone?" cried Susan, who was itching to be off.

"I can't go like this," Bill said and began to tear off his shirt of crêpe paper streamers, "but you mustn't go without me! Susie, wait for me, promise you'll wait for me!"

"You'd think it was your grandfather we were worrying about," said Midge.

Mr. Dean said mildly, "Hadn't we better have dinner now and then call on this Mrs.—what's her name?—to-morrow? After all—"

"Well, I couldn't eat a bite," said Susan, "wondering about it, could you, Mr. Dean, honestly?"

Mr. Dean said rather apologetically that he thought he could.

"Oh well," said Susan, nearly crying with disappointment, "it's your relations really, I suppose, Mr. Dean, so you must wait till to-morrow if you want to—" and she turned away, because really Mr. Dean was jolly decent and she didn't want him to see her howling like a baby.

But this was too much for kind-hearted Mr. Dean. "Well," he said weakly, "let's see what your aunt has to say about it—"

"Oh, Aunt Lucy will never wait until to-morrow if there's a mystery to be solved," said Midge. "Come on, Susie, let's go and tell her—"

"I'm ready, I'm ready!" A sort of piebald ex-witch doctor burst out of his room; a shirt and grey shorts had been pulled on, a towel had been hastily and not very expertly rubbed over himself, leaving streaks of black greasepaint.

"Mr. Dean thinks we should wait until to-morrow," said Midge.

At Bill's expression, coming on top of Susan's deliberately turned back, Mr. Dean felt lower than a creeping worm. He said quickly, "We're going to ask your aunt what she thinks—"

There wasn't much doubt about what Aunt Lucy thought. She pushed them all into Uncle Charles's car and started up the engine before they knew what was happening. "I hope your daddy doesn't have an emergency call," she muttered.

Charlotte came flying out of the house, calling and waving. "Well!" she said, "I like that, going off without me! Where are you all going?"

Susan explained in a quick gabble.

"Well, push over," said Charlotte, "and let me in. Going off without me!" Susan obligingly made room on the back seat and Charlotte squeezed in.

"I thought you had a date with a ghastly Gascoigne?" Midge murmured.

"Oh, he can wait," said Charlotte grandly.

Midge and Susan grinned at each other. That was more like it. Then Midge said, "Are we all going to crowd in on Mrs. Thorne? She'll have a heart attack."

"Oh well, I must go in," said Bill, "because I have the lion's skin—"

"I actually borrowed it," said Midge, "so I ought to take it back—"

"I'm the eldest—" Charlotte began, although she didn't think that she honestly had a very good case.

"*I* must go in," said Aunt Lucy, teasing them, "because I bought her a hot-water bottle cover at the fête—"

Poor Susan was in agony. She would simply die if she didn't get inside the little house to ask about James Martin, but she really couldn't think of any reason why she should. *She* hadn't found the clue, *she* hadn't found Mr. Dean's relations, in fact *she*—

"And Susie must go in—" it was Midge saying the blessed word, "because she always rushes in—"

Gavin Dean laughed. "I suggest that Miss Carmichael and I wait in the car," he said, "while you four go in—"

Mrs. Thorne, as usual, seemed pleased to see them. She was delighted with her hot-water bottle cover too, and Susan, hopping from foot to foot, thought that these polite preliminaries would go on all night. "Mrs. Thorne," she burst in when she couldn't stand it any longer, "we're most frightfully interested in your lion's skin and this that's written on it saying that James Martin shot it, and we were wondering very much if you could tell us anything about this James Martin and where you got the lion's skin—"

"I can tell you plenty about James Martin," said Mrs. Thorne smiling, "because he was my brother!"

CHAPTER TWELVE

AT THE ELEVENTH HOUR

THERE WAS an uproar of rejoicing.

"But—but—but—then Mrs. Thorne *is* Mr. Dean's relations!" Susan stammered happily if not very grammatically. "I thought Mrs. Thorne might know something *about* his relations, I never thought that she would *be* his relations!"

"Mrs. Thorne is his grandmother or something," cried Bill.

"Grand-*aunt*, you owl—," said Charlotte.

Midge tried to say that it might not be the same James Martin, but no one paid any attention to her. So she went and sat down in Mrs. Thorne's most comfortable chair and lay back. It looked as though this was going to take a bit of sorting out, so she might as well sit down to it, she thought.

Mrs. Thorne said, "What are you young people talking—indeed *yelling*—about?"

"We'll tell you—" said Susan.

She led Mrs. Thorne gently to a chair and sent Bill to the kitchen for some water—just in case, as she tactfully put it. Bill, with a huge jug of water slopping all over the floor, tore back in case he missed anything. Susan held Mrs. Thorne's hand and gave it gentle little pats. All these precautions and preparations were by this time getting Mrs. Thorne into quite a state of agitation. "If it's bad news," she said quite sharply, "just tell me and have done with it!"

"It's not *bad* news, Mrs. Thorne!" exclaimed Susan. "We hope it's frightfully good news. But we don't want you to faint with joy."

"I never fainted in my life," said Mrs. Thorne, her brown eyes snapping, "and I'm not likely to begin now—"

"Well, Mrs. Thorne," said Susan, her always rosy cheeks blazing with excitement, "it's like this—"

"Oh get *on*, Susie," said Midge in her laziest voice, "I'm nearly asleep—"

Susan, who liked to savour the full drama of a situation, glanced at Midge reproachfully, took a deep breath and giving Mrs. Thorne's hand another little pat, she said, "Well, Mrs. Thorne, you know our friend Mr. Dean who came from South Africa— ?"

"No," said Mrs. Thorne, "I don't, but I know who you mean."

"Yes, well, our Mr. Dean's grandfather's name was James Martin, and we think that he was your brother!"

Mrs. Thorne looked at her sharply and eagerly for a second, then the eagerness went out of her eyes and she shook her head. "My brother James had only one child, a daughter, and she married a man called du Toit or some such outlandish name. Then my brother died and his wife died and I got married and moved away from Wichwood and I never heard of my niece again. I wrote more than once, but my letters always came back marked 'Not known at this address '."

Susan was nearly sick with disappointment. She took the jug of water from Bill who was still clutching it and took a drink—but it didn't make her feel any better, worse if anything—she just *couldn't* bear to think of those letters coming back unanswered to the poor lonely old lady.

Then Midge's voice broke the silence. "Why don't you get Mr. Dean?" she said. "It's *his* great-aunt after all. Or not, as the case may be—"

Susan darted out to the car, babbling. "Oh Mr. Dean, *do* you think you could come in, because first we thought that Mrs. Thorne was your great-aunt or grand-aunt or whatever you call it, and then we thought she wasn't because her niece was called Mrs. du Toit and not your mother—"

"Susan!" Aunt Lucy exclaimed at the sight and sound of her niece. "Are you feeling all right?"

"Yes, of course, Aunt Lucy," said Susan.

"Well you look to me as though you had a fever—!"

"Och, Aunt Lucy, *honestly*!" said Susan, and added, "But I will have, if Mr. Dean doesn't come in and settle all this—!"

Mr. Dean obligingly came in, followed by Aunt Lucy, who felt that she had missed quite enough of the excitement already, and she introduced Mr. Dean to old Mrs. Thorne, and before Susan could put her oar in, muddling everybody up, Mrs. Thorne said in her rather precise old voice, "How do you do, Mr. Dean. The young people tell me that you come from South Africa and that your grandfather's name was James Martin. That was also my brother's name, but as he had only one child, a daughter who married a man called du Toit, I fear that we cannot be connected after all—"

Gavin Dean said with a kind of excitement about him too, "But I think we are, because my mother was married twice and her first husband's name was du Toit!"

So then there was a great deal of quiet rejoicing, and some more noisy rejoicing from Susan and Bill and Mrs. Thorne could hardly believe that she had found a great-nephew, and the talk flew between her and Gavin Dean, with Charlotte and Bill and Aunt Lucy and Susan putting in a word when they had the chance, and Midge repeating over and over again in a quiet voice, "Well, this is all absolutely thrilling and marvellous, but what about our dinner?" until at last Aunt Lucy heard her.

"Oh, and the car too, what will your father say!" she exclaimed, and jumped guiltily to her feet. "Well of course it's much too late to go careering away up to town now, we'll all just go home and have scrambled eggs after all—"

Of course Mrs. Thorne came too, and it was quite a squash in the car, but as they approached The Willows Charlotte said "Adrian!" in a guilty voice and begged Aunt Lucy to let her off. And Aunt Lucy said what about supper and Charlotte said that she would have something there, at the dance, that there were to be hot dogs and things like that. So there was more room in the car for the last little bit down Tollgate Road, past the lovely old Georgian houses and the wide grass verges with the railings and white-painted posts round them. When they reached home they found that Uncle Charles, far from stamping up and down shouting for his car, had gone next door to ask the Gascoignes if they knew anything about his family and had stayed there for dinner. This upset Midge and Bill and Susan very much—first Charlotte and now Daddy off in the camp of the enemy.

"The only revenge I can think of," said Susan viciously, "will be to get Gavin Dean to do something to spike horrid Mr. Pilkington's guns. Surely he'll do something about that—tell a lawyer what Mr. Pilkington is planning to do to his aunt and have him put in prison—"

Midge said, "I don't think that what horrid Mr. Pilkington is doing is actually the kind of thing you get put in prison for, only bad and horrible— but perhaps at least Mr. Dean will be able to find Mrs. Thorne a nicer place to live than that room in Cox's Grove which I must say sounded nasty to a degree although dear Mrs. Thorne was trying to make the best of it—"

"We must tell Mr. Dean *now*," cried Susan. "The minute we get a chance—!"

Their chance came quite soon. After supper, Mrs. Thorne confessed that she *did* feel a little tired, only with a nice kind of tiredness, and Aunt Lucy took her home in the car. The minute that she was out of the door, Susan rushed to Mr. Dean and said, "Mr. Dean, we thought you ought to know that your aunt is going to be put out of her house very soon!"

Gavin Dean looked startled and said, "What *do* you mean?"

"Well," said Susan, "your aunt's landlord is going

to sell her house to horrid Mr. Pilkington who lives next door so that he can build on a studio or a bathroom or something—"

"Although I must say," Midge put in, "he doesn't look as if he used the bathroom he's got, far less build another."

"But where's my aunt going to live ?" said Gavin Dean.

"In a horrid little furnished room," said Susan, dramatising as usual, "that doesn't get any sun—!"

"But does my aunt want to go to this one room ?" Gavin Dean demanded.

"Och, of course she doesn't! She's as sick as mud at leaving her sweet little house and all her nice things, because of course there won't be space in the horrible furnished room for even her favourite tea-set!" cried Susan, Mrs. Thorne's furnished room becoming smaller and smaller in her mind's eye as she talked. "You see, it was very difficult for her finding even a room because it seems that people who let rooms don't want old ladies in case they get ill on their hands—"

Gavin Dean looked grim. "But this landlord," he said, "surely he can't just push her out like that ?"

"Well, he did give her the chance of buying the house," said Midge, "but naturally she couldn't because she hasn't any money—"

"He gave her until the ninth of this month," said Susan, "but she told us this morning that now she had found a room she would tell him on Monday to carry on and sell the house to horrid Mr. Pilkington. She was going to tell him to-day but we persuaded her to wait till Monday—gosh!" she exclaimed, suddenly realising just how narrow the time margin had been, "that was a narrow squak, wasn't it! We must have had a pre- pre- whatever you call it that something would turn up!" She looked at the others, wide-eyed. "I *did* say that something would turn up, didn't I ?"

Gavin Dean said, "Where does this landlord live ? D'you know his name ?"

"His name is Hart and he lives in the village. I know him very well," said Bill, who should have been in bed but who had been allowed to sit up late in honour of the touching family reunion. "He's a jolly nice old boy and I'm sure he didn't want to sell the house over Mrs. Thorne's head, but he needed the money, he said—"

Gavin Dean rose from his chair. "Well, come on—!" he said.

"Come on where ?" asked Susan, stupidly.

"To see this Mr. Hart, of course," said Gavin Dean. "He won't be in bed, will he ?"

"Well, he's rather an ancient old party," Bill said, "but I shouldn't think that even he would be in bed by eight o'clock. After all, *I'm* not in bed and I'm only eleven—"

"Let's go, then," said Gavin Dean.

This was a man after Susan's own heart. They hastily scribbled a note for Aunt Lucy and accompanied Mr. Dean to the village, to the rather prim Georgian house where Mr. Hart lived. "Wait here," said Gavin Dean. He ran up the short flight of steps to the door, rang the bell and disappeared into the house.

He was out again in less than ten minutes, beaming. "Well, that's that settled!" he said.

"What did you do, Mr. Dean?" asked Susan.

"Bought the house, of course," said Gavin Dean.

Susan and Midge and Bill were all absolutely thrilled, but Susan couldn't help wondering what Mr. Dean was going to do about money. "But Mr. Dean," she faltered, "the money! Horrid Mr. Pilkington was offering a thousand pounds!"

"Yes, well," said Gavin Dean carelessly, "I've given Mr. Hart one thousand two hundred for luck—" Then seeing their astonished faces he smiled and said, "Didn't you know that I'm quite disgustingly rich? I made pots of money on that film they made from one of my books—so I can easily afford to buy a little house for my only great-aunt. Besides, I wanted somewhere to live for a year or two when I'm in England and now I've got it—"

"Oh that's all right then," cried Susan in great relief. "Oh *how* blissful everything is!"

"*And* one in the eye for horrid Mr. Pilkington and the ghastly Gascoignes," said Midge with deep satisfaction.

"Jolly nice having you in Wichwood, sir," said Bill gruffly.

They started to walk back through the village under the heavy shadows of the chestnuts and the lime trees, and Gavin Dean looked pleased. "D'you think that my aunt will have me to stay with her?" he said.

"Och, of *course*," said Susan, who hadn't the least

idea, really, but who was determined that everybody should be happy.

Midge, who knew Mrs. Thorne rather better, said with conviction, "She'll adore having someone of her own to fuss over and bake gingerbread for. But I do think you ought to get someone in to do the rough, Mr. Dean, because a man in the house makes a lot of work, our Aunt Lucy says, and Mrs. Thorne is rather old you know."

"I know," said Mr. Dean soberly. "But don't worry, I'll look after her all right." He suddenly said, "By the way, do any of you happen to know her name?"

"Well, Mrs. Thorne of course," said Susan. She thought that was one thing that everybody knew.

"Her Christian name, you dope," said Midge.

But nobody knew Mrs. Thorne's Christian name, and they giggled all the way home at Mr. Dean's having a new aunt and not even knowing her name!

CHAPTER THIRTEEN

A NEW CAREER FOR CHARLOTTE

FOR THE next few days, the Gascoignes showed a distinct coolness towards the Carmichaels. "Mad as snakes about Mrs. Thorne's little house being snatched from horrid Mr. Pilkington's grasp at the eleventh hour," said Midge with glee. Gossip in the village said that Mr. Pilkington was absolutely furious and this was verified by Pat Murphy when Susan and Midge and Bill encountered him in the village a few days later. "A sight for sore eyes it was," he said, "when the ould gentleman told Mr. Sam Pilkington that the house was sold. Sold, is it, sez he, I'll have the law on ye, sez he, and kicked over a bucket of paint in his rage. And I'll have the law on *ye*, sez the ould gentleman, for the paint went all over his trousers, and I was just going to join in the fight meself when that Mrs. Gascoigne from number twelve next door to yourselves stepped in the door and spoilt all the fun!"

"So you won't be going to Mrs. Thorne's little house to pull it to pieces," said Susan.

"Not to be pulling it to pieces, no, but did you not hear that Mrs. Thorne's house is to be painted from top to bottom ? So when I'm in there I'll be having a look-out for that little bit of a miser's hoard I was telling you about!"

"Mrs. Thorne says that there *was* a miser and a

miser's hoard, Mr. Murphy, but that he put it in the post office," said Bill, who didn't want his friend to be disappointed.

"Och now, isn't that the provoking ould miser he is, to be doing a thing like that instead of leaving his hoard for a poor man to find! But mebbe there will be a wee little bit of money that he overlooked when he was putting it in the post office—I'll be keeping a sharp look-out for it—"

For Mr. Dean was taking his great-aunt (whose name turned out to be Emily) for jaunts all over the place and was planning to take her to Devon for a little holiday, and while they were away the house was to be painted. There was no doubt about Mrs. Thorne's delight at the idea of Gavin's living with her—she had lavender-scented sheets on the spare-room bed before you could say knife, and the sitting-room reorganiscd for him with a table for his typewriter and strictest orders given to the daily woman from the village who had been engaged as Midge suggested ' to do the rough ' that she must not disturb him on any account when he was in there working at his writing. Susan was in the seventh heaven, suggesting to Gavin Dean ways of pleasing Great-aunt Emily, and it was just as well, she said gloomily, that one of their problems was going well, because the other was anything *but*. Of course the fact that the Gascoignes seemed to be offended with them over the part they had played in thwarting horrid Mr. Pilkington was a great help, if only they could keep it going, but they had been plunged in despair at least twice by overhearing Uncle Charles asking Aunt Lucy what had happened to little Mrs. Gascoigne recently, he hadn't seen her about for days.

And as for Charlotte—words could not express the disgust of Midge and Susan and Bill over Charlotte's on-goings. Archaeology was one thing, they felt, but the archaeologist was quite another—when he was a hated Gascoigne. She even brought Adrian into the house—which couldn't have been very comfortable for him because Midge and Bill and Susan sat glaring at him solidly, although they were later forced to admit that he was possibly the best of the three.

"Of the four!" said Bill. "He's much better than That Woman!"

"But don't you *hate* the affected way he calls her Mama ?" said Midge. "I hate that almost as much as the way the others call her Selina. And Aunt Lucy beaming because at *last* one of us likes a ghastly Gascoigne and Daddy saying he seems a nice boy, with something in his head, not like most of the young men one meets nowadays—!"

"All he has in his head is Greek remains and a hot potato in his mouth," said Susan scornfully. "You know, the fact of the matter is," she went on humbly, "I haven't been much help after all, I haven't thought of a single scheme to get rid of the Gascoignes or to disgrace them in Uncle Charles's eyes, in fact he only likes them better after every encounter!"

"Oh Susie, my pet, don't go all modest and despairing on us at this stage," said Midge. "All your energies should be bent on keeping the Gascoignes at arm's length or even farther. And although I dare say that Mrs. Thorne would have found Gavin *eventually*, I'm sure that horrid Mr. Pilkington would have had her house by that time if you hadn't rushed in."

This kind and encouraging speech cheered Susan up very much, but not for long, for Charlotte went banging out of the house just then, and Midge and Susan and Bill stood at the window and with gloomy rage watched Charlotte, all done up in her best clothes too, going up Tollgate Road by the side of Adrian.

"Taking her to the British Museum!" said Midge scornfully. "To show her Greek remains! She can go to the British Museum by herself, can't she ?"

"Or we could have gone with her," said Bill. "I shouldn't mind seeing some remains."

"I don't think these remains are quite what you think they are," said Midge, "but she still didn't need Adrian to show them to her. They're all laid out in glass cases with tickets on them. Anybody can see them—"

"And taking her to see that Roman temple that was dug up in the City," said Bill, "*I'd* have liked to see that—"

"And that lecture on archæology he took her to," said Susan. "I bet she went to sleep in the middle of that, because I asked her what it was about and she couldn't tell me. Said I wouldn't understand. What is there about archæology I wouldn't understand, I'd like to know ? After all, we had a dig, hadn't we, Bill ? We found our knife, didn't we, Bill ?"

For the knife, while perhaps not qualifying as

archæological remains, as Susan would be the first to admit, had turned out to be quite old, an early eighteenth-century knife. Mrs. Gascoigne had sent it in with a note to say that her friend at the British Museum had been most interested and that was what he said it was.

"We got it back well after the exhibition of Home Curiosities, you remember," said Susan broodingly. She thought that she would never get over the disappointment of not having their knife in the exhibition. Not to mention the chance of the guinea prize that had been missed. "That Pea-green and his grain of rice!"

"Well, it doesn't matter now," said Midge soothingly, "we don't need the money now."

"No, now that we don't need the money it pours in," agreed Susan, in a slightly exaggerated way.

For even in the excitement of finding a great-aunt, Gavin had not forgotten about *The Story of the Treasure-Seekers*. In fact he had renewed his offer to buy the book from Midge and Susan for six pounds. Midge and Susan had a discussion about it. "Now that Mrs. Thorne's house is going to be painted all over, I should think that bit we damaged will be included and we shan't get the bill sent to us after all," said Midge.

"You mean, we shouldn't take the six pounds for *The Story of the Treasure-Seekers* ?" asked Susan.

"Well, we don't actually need the money now," said Midge.

"Money's always useful," said Susan. "Going to Switzerland and everything—"

Midge agreed. "All the same," she went on,

"don't you think that we ought to make him a present of it, if he's so keen on it?"

They finally decided that that would be the nicest thing to do; but to their great delight, Gavin Dean simply refused to accept such a valuable gift. He finally agreed to split the difference and gave them three pounds for it; and Aunt Lucy telephoned Mrs. Mountford-Jones and Mrs. Mountford-Jones hadn't the slightest idea who had sent the book to the second-hand book-stall, so there was nothing that Susan's tender conscience could do about that, although she did suggest advertising. Now that they were women of means, Midge and Susan took Bill up to town to buy him a new copy of *The Story of the Treasure-Seekers*. Bill said that if it was all the same to them he'd rather have a book called *Model-making for Boys*, but Midge and Susan were firm, it was *The Story of the Treasure-Seekers* or nothing. So Bill graciously accepted it, and as a matter of fact in time it became one of his favourite books, too.

So financially at least things were quite rosy, and as it happened even more money was on the way, for on Friday morning a letter came. It was addressed, rather mysteriously, to Miss Marjorie Charlotte Carmichael. Midge and Susan and Bill were hanging over it, wondering whom it was really for, when Charlotte appeared at the breakfast table with two books on archaeology lent by Adrian under her arm.

"Some dotty ass has written to Miss Marjorie Charlotte Carmichael," said Midge. "Shall I open—"

Before she had finished speaking, Charlotte cried, "Oh, they've written!" grabbed the letter, looked at the name on the back, tore it open with her finger, a habit she had which aggravated the rest of the family, and read it. Then she sat down suddenly, with her mouth open, looking quite pale, and let the letter flutter on to the table. "Well!" she said. "Ten guineas!"

Susan picked up the letter. "Read it out!" said Midge. "Who's it from ? What does it say ?"

"It's from some firm called Hamilton Press, type-written too," said Susan, "and it says: ' Dear Miss Carmichael, I liked your story, THE GREEDY DRAGON, very much, and should like to have it for our list. I can offer you an outright payment of ten guineas, which I hope will be satisfactory. If you have any other stories along the same lines and using the same dragon character in mind, I should be glad to see them, with a view to building up a small series.' And it's signed, ' T. I. S. Harrison Children's Book Editor '!"

"Goodness!" said Midge. "What on earth does it mean ?"

Charlotte said, still in a dazed voice, "Well, it's from a publisher, and he's going to publish your story about the dragon that ate little boys and give us ten guineas for it!"

"He must be off his rocker," said Midge. "And anyway, how did he get it ?"

Charlotte blushed. "Mrs. Gascoigne gave it to him," she said uncomfortably. Midge and Susan and Bill drew themselves up at the hated name and Charlotte rushed on, "Wait, and I'll tell you. You know I was scribbling away at dragons after Midge wrote her story—yes, well then I thought they'd look rather fun in a little book, so I put them into a little sort of book with the story written out in script. And then I thought, Selina seems to know all about everything, I'll show it to her, and she said that she had a friend who published children's books and she'd let him see it—so she has, I suppose, and he's going to publish it and pay us ten guineas for it!"

"Us ?" asked Midge, anxious to know. "Me too ?"

"Well of course, us," said Charlotte, "you wrote the story and I did the pictures, so I called us Marjorie Charlotte Carmichael."

Bill and Susan were still staring at Midge and Charlotte as if they were some strange kind of animal. "Fancy!" said Susan at last. "Having a book published, and you're only fourteen!"

"As a matter of fact," said Midge, in an embarrassed way, "I've always hated books written by people in their teens and wouldn't read them on principle. But no one needs to know how old we are, do they, Charlotte ?" Charlotte said no, no, in a soothing way and Midge went on in a frightened voice, "And now do I have to sit and write stories about dragons all day ?"

"Och away," said Susan, "you did that one in about five minutes! Fancy, ten guineas for five minutes' work!"

"Five guineas," said Midge. "Charlotte gets half, don't forget."

When Aunt Lucy and Uncle Charles came in to breakfast and heard the news they were speechless with amazement too for a minute, then quite bursting with pride.

"There!" said Aunt Lucy. "I was right! I always wanted you to be an artist, Charlotte—!"

"Yes, well, even now I'm not going to be an *artist* actually," said Charlotte, "but I should like to be a book illustrator, I always said so, and I don't mind going somewhere and taking classes and learning how to do it when I've left school—"

"I hope nobody wants me to be a writer!" said Midge in alarm. "Sitting writing day after day, I'd die!"

"Oh well," Aunt Lucy laughed, "we don't need to worry about that yet."

"But you'll do some more dragon stories!" cried Susan. "It would be awful to let the chance of earning lots of lovely guineas slip through your fingers!"

"If I can think of another," said Midge, looking slightly hunted already.

Dr. Carmichael just couldn't get over it. He read and re-read Mr. Harrison's letter. "Of course, your grandfather used to write a bit, Midge," he said, "and he was editor of the Glasgow Medical Journal, too, so perhaps you take after him. But we certainly never had an artist in the family before, as far as I know. You must go in and tell Mrs. Gascoigne, of course, and thank her for all the trouble that she has taken. She never said a word about it when I saw her last night—"

It was a thousand pities that this great success had come to them at the hands of That Woman, they felt, as they all trailed next door to see Mrs. Gascoigne.

"Don't you think that we're almost as interesting, amusing, original and clever as the ghastly Gascoignes," Midge said, "now that we write books ?"

"You'll never be as amusing as Pea-green, thank goodness," said Susan.

Mrs. Gascoigne was all sweetness when they went in—their part in the Thorne-Pilkington affair must have been forgiven, they thought. She was delighted that her friend Tizzy Harrison as she called him was going to publish the dragon book, she herself thought it was such fun, and would they all come to a *tiny* party next evening, she was sorry that it was such short notice, but she had only decided to have it at twelve o'clock the previous night ?

"That'll teach us to go calling on That Woman," Midge grumbled as they returned home. "Now we're back where we started, everybody great friends with the ghastly Gascoignes and Daddy—" but that didn't bear thinking about, so she tried not to think about it, but tried instead to think about *The Greedy Dragon*. My story is going to be published, she thought, put in a real book with Marjorie Charlotte Carmichael on the outside, but she still couldn't believe it, although it gave her a little warm glow inside, especially when she remembered the guineas. And it was at least some consolation, as she pointed out to Susan, to see the effect of Mr. Tizzy Harrison's letter on Charlotte. For Charlotte spent the morning with the archæological tomes beside her, it's true, but she was using them to rest her drawing block on while dragons flowed from her pencil.

At eleven o'clock Mr. Dean came with his vast car to take them all for a drive as he had promised because he was selling it next day and buying a smaller one to take Mrs. Thorne to Devon. Aunt Lucy wanted him to see the Carmichaels' favourite little corner of Kent—round Otford and Shoreham and Eynsford, returning by Farthing Green. Aunt Lucy had been talking to him about it and telling him about their friends who lived in the old mill house at Farthing Green and how last Easter Susan had found an aunt for them too.*

Gabrielle and Peregrine just happened to come out of their house while everybody was milling round Mr. Dean's huge car, and Mr. Dean asked them if they would like to come too. They expressed great delight and ran in to tell their mother.

"How many are coming ?" muttered Bill, wondering what his chances of sitting in front with Mr. Dean were now that the car was going to be filled up with ghastly Gascoignes. "There won't be room—"

"Oh, Bill, it's a huge car," said Aunt Lucy. "And only Gabrielle and Peregrine are coming—"

"I suppose that's why they came out," said Midge. "To cadge an invitation. Well, I can only hope that they clean up a bit before they come—"

"Midge—" Aunt Lucy began in a dangerous voice, but Bill butted in and managed to arrange to sit in the front with Aunt Lucy and Mr. Dean before Gabrielle and Peregrine, both exceedingly grubby and untidy, charged out of the house.

"Oh help!" said Susan. "Such sights! I'd be ashamed to be seen with them! We'll have to stay in the car all the time!"

* See " Susan's Helping Hand."

"'Mm," Midge said. "Or walk behind them and pretend we're not with them."

Under Aunt Lucy's direction, they drove through rather dull suburbs to the valley of the Darent, through the lovely villages of Otford and Shoreham and Eynsford. Mr. Dean was enchanted. It was all he had ever pictured England to be, he said, and he got out of the car and stared at half-timbered houses and ancient inns and cottage gardens going down to little clear streams that hurried through the villages and tall church spires calmly overlooking village greens. And in return the villagers stared at Mr. Dean's car.

They had lunch at a converted oast-house, and Aunt Lucy tried to tidy Gabrielle and Peregrine up in order to appear in public. These efforts were rather rudely swept aside by Gabrielle and Peregrine —Selina *never* made them wash their hands or tidy their hair if they didn't want to—and Aunt Lucy said mildly, oh well, what Mrs. Gascoigne did was one thing, but as far as she was concerned, nobody had lunch until hands had been washed and hair combed. Peregrine stared at her with his big dark eyes and said did she know that she might be doing terrible damage to their egos, that she might be setting up a washing-resistance that he and Gabrielle might never get over ? Midge muttered under her breath that their washing-resistance seemed pretty well established already, and Aunt Lucy laughed and said that she would have to chance that, and would they please pop off and *wash*.

As the party was returning from Shoreham on the way to Farthing Green, Susan, who did not like to miss anything, ever, drew attention to a signpost which pointed the way to Lullingstone Castle. "What sort of a place is Lullingstone Castle?" she asked. "Is it an old castle?"

"Yes," said Aunt Lucy, "it is, but what it mainly is now is a silkworm farm."

"Do please let's go," said Midge, "we haven't been for simply ages."

"Silkworms?" said Peregrine. "We *must* go and see silkworms—"

If he had only known it, this way of talking was enough to put Aunt Lucy off completely, but she knew that her own family loved a visit to the silkworms and that Susan had never been. "Well," she said, "if Mr. Dean—"

Mr. Dean said that there was nothing he would like better than to visit a silkworm farm, he hadn't seen a silkworm since he was aged ten at his prep school, in Johannesburg. In those days he had kept silkworms every year—in fact he had made quite a good thing out of selling silkworms, reaching, that last year when he was ten, the record total of four and sevenpence.

So in view of this general interest in silkworms, they took the turning off the main road towards Lullingstone Castle.

They passed the great Tudor gateway and the little white church on the grass and went into the great hall of the castle where parties assembled, waiting to be conducted round the various stages in the production of silk. As it was a week-day, there were very few people waiting when the Carmichaels' party arrived—just a couple of earnest young men on a cycling trip and a harassed mother with three children, all of whom, as Susan whispered to Midge, were going to resemble Pea-green closely in behaviour when they were a little older. They were all sucking lollipops and their general appearance was sticky and adenoidal. A pleasant young woman in an overall arrived to conduct the tour and everyone moved off in her wake through a heavy door into a big bare apartment where on long trestle tables millions of silkworms were gorging happily on mulberry leaves.

"Jings!" exclaimed Susan, and gazed fascinated at these voracious creatures.

The young woman explained about the silkworms' diet, which was mulberry leaves, specially grown for them in the grounds, and Peregrine, who was right at the very front of the little crowd of sightseers, shamed and mortified Susan and the Carmichaels by announcing in his high voice that he had kept silkworms for years and had fed them on an exclusive diet of lettuce on which they thrived exceedingly. The girl, looking slightly amused, said that you *could* rear silkworms on lettuce, even on beetroot, although mulberry leaves were best, but one thing you couldn't do was change their diet in the middle, switch lettuce eaters on to mulberry and vice versa because then the silkworms died. Peregrine piped up again with some other profound observation and Susan, embarrassed for him, tore off her blazer and whispered to Midge, "I'm absolutely *boiling*!"

"Well, no wonder," murmured Midge, "didn't you hear what she said? They have to keep the temperature away up in the eighties."

"Oh help, did she ?" said Susan. "I thought it was Pea-green making me hot all over—" She put her blazer down on a low windowsill and felt better.

They followed the career of the silkworms through their various stages, from the eating stage to the neatly wound little cocoons of silk, to the moths and the egg-laying stage; and between the sticky family, who liked to poke the silkworms with their lollipops, and Peregrine with his questions, in was a wonder that the girl remained so calm and patient. Latterly, however, much to Susan's and Midge's relief, Peregrine and his questions rather faded out.

On their way to the shed where the silk was wound off the cocoons, they came out into the open air and Susan shivered. "Goodness, it's cold after that hot-house atmosphere," she said.

"Put on your blazer, then," said Midge.

"My blazer ? My blazer! I've left it behind!" cried Susan. "Oh blow!"

"Better go back and get it then," said Midge.

"Oh, do come with me," said Susan.

"Trail all the way back through all those rooms ?" said Midge faintly.

"Och, it's not far!" said Susan, smiling at her.

"Well, I suppose I'd better," said Midge, "or you'll be getting lost and those savage silkworms might attack you—"

They found the blazer without mishap and caught up with the rest of the party in the shed watching the silk being reeled off the cocoons, which were bobbing about in water. Susan said, "The smell! Isn't it awful!"

"Revolting," Midge agreed. "And the noise of the machines! Let's get out of here—!"

They went outside, and stood leaning up against the wall while the rest of the party of sightseers, having gazed their fill at the winding-machines, clattered up a wooden stair to see some further stage in the evolution of the silk. Midge took a deep breath. "Heavens, I hated the stink in there," she said. "What's that crawling on your blazer?" she went on, idly.

Susan glanced down at her blazer. "That white thing?" she said. "It's a— Midge! It's a silkworm! How did that get there?"

"It came out of your pocket," said Midge.

"Yes, but how did it get into my pocket?" said Susan agitatedly. She thrust her hand into her pocket, where it met a damp, soft mass. "Midge!" she exclaimed. "My pocket is full of something—" she brought out her hand and exhibited a mingled mess of mulberry leaves and silkworms. "Oh gosh!" she said. "They must have crawled into my pocket when my blazer was left in that room!"

"And I suppose the leaves crawled into your pocket too," said Midge, "or d'you imagine that the silkworms took their dinner with them?"

Susan was much too unnerved to be upset by this sarcasm. "Oh gosh, Midge," she said, "supposing that girl sees them! She'll think I pinched them! Gosh I must take them back—!"

"Susie, don't be such an ass," said Midge. "They'll never miss a couple of silkworms out of all those millions."

"A couple!" Susan exclaimed. "There are

hundreds in my pocket! I must put them back!
I'm sure that they're all counted! The whole industry might be upset if I don't—!"

Midge thought that this was a bit unlikely, but
nothing would do but that Susan must return the
silkworms. Midge reluctantly agreed, and together
they cautiously made their way once more to the
first room that they had visited, through the heavy
doors. Susan began gingerly to empty her pocket
and to replace the errant silkworms on their trays.
"Och," she said, "these little blighters don't half
cling," and she tried gently but firmly to dislodge the
silkworms from her blazer pocket.

The door opened and the girl who had shown them
round came in. "What are you girls doing ?" she
asked sharply.

Susan jumped about a foot in the air, blushed
furiously and stammered, "N-n-nothing," she said.

"You weren't helping yourself to a few silkworms
by any chance ?"

"On the contrary," Midge murmured under her
breath.

"No, of course not!" Susan exclaimed, looking
the picture of guilt.

The girl stared at her hard, "Well, you shouldn't
be in here by yourselves," she said. "Off you go—"

Midge and Susan went. Out in the great hall
Susan whispered in a worried voice, "But I've still
got *masses* of silkworms in my pocket!"

"Well, that's just bad luck for the silk industry,"
said Midge. "But I'm not going back into that
room for all the silk in China. And neither are
you—"

They found the rest of their party searching for them round the grounds. "Oh, there you are," said Charlotte, "we thought you'd been eaten by silkworms."

They moved off over the little bridge towards the car-park and the car and Peregrine came rushing up. "Oh, there you are!" he said in his turn. "I was beginning to get anxious—" He came up to Susan and put his hand into her pocket. "I hope you haven't squashed them," he said severely.

Susan wanted to haul Peregrine before the Lullingstone Castle authorities and denounce him, and said so. Gabrielle said scornfully, "Surely you're not going to be a sneak and *tell*, are you? I thought that was one of the things that simply weren't done at your absurd public schools?"

Susan muttered furiously under her breath, but when Aunt Lucy and Gavin Dean joined them she said nothing. "I'll be revenged on that Pea-green yet," she muttered to Midge.

But unfortunately, her insatiable desire to be helping, rescuing and poking her nose generally into the affairs of others, even silkworms, got the better of her again, even before any ideas for revenge could take effect. After tea, when Mr. Dean had taken himself and his glorious car back to his Aunt Emily's, and the Gascoignes were safely in their own house again, Susan suddenly said dramatically, as she and Midge were washing up the tea-things together, "They'll die!"

"If you mean the ghastly Gascoignes," said Midge,

sketchily drying a tea-cup and hanging it on its hook, " the sooner the better."

"Och, of course I don't mean the Gascoignes," said Susan. "I mean the silkworms."

"I shouldn't worry about the silkworms," said Midge. "That's Pea-green's worry. He can feed his ill-gotten gain along with his own silkworms—"

"That's just what I'm afraid of!" said Susan. "And they'll die! Don't you remember what that girl said ? If you start feeding silkworms that have been brought up on mulberry leaves on lettuce, then they'll die!"

Midge looked singularly unmoved. "They *must* have mulberry leaves!" Susan went on. "I must find them some mulberry leaves! But I don't know where there are any mulberry trees!"

"As a matter of fact," said Midge, "there are mulberry trees in the Gallery garden."

Opposite the Carmichaels' house there was a small but quite famous picture gallery. The Carmichaels —naturally, seeing that they lived opposite—had scarcely ever been in it, but as children their nanny had often taken them into the very pretty garden which surrounded it.

"Well that's a bit of luck!" cried Susan. "I must tell Pea-green—"

Midge refused to have anything further to do with the Gascoignes that day—or any day for that matter —as she had enough of *them* she said, to last her a lifetime. She also refused to let Susan off the rest of the washing-up in order to rush in and remind Pea-green about the silkworms' diet. However, she couldn't do anything to stop her going next door after the washing-up was finished. But when Susan knocked at the Gascoignes' front door and inquired for Peregrine, Gabrielle said that he was in bed.

"Stomach-ache again?" said Susan tactlessly.

Gabrielle looked at her coldly. "Peregrine is a very highly strung and temperamental child," she said. "All the excitement to-day has made him sick."

Susan didn't think that Pea-green had had nearly such an exciting day as she had had—who had had all the worry of the blessed silkworms anyway? Still, Pea-green's temperaments weren't her concern, luckily.

"What about his silkworms?" she said.

"Well, *what* about them?" said Gabrielle.

"I mean, are they all right, or have they got stomach-ache—I mean, are they over-excited too?" said Susan.

"I suppose you think you're frightfully witty?" said Gabrielle.

Susan had thought that she was being *rather* funny, but she said hurriedly, "Och of course not, Gabrielle, only I was rather worried about the silk worms that Pea-green stole because they ought to have mulberry leaves—"

"I think we can safely leave the question of the silkworms' food to Peregrine, don't you?" said Gabrielle in her most irritating grown-up manner. "After all, he has been keeping silkworms for years and does know rather a lot about them."

"Well, don't you think we can?" said Midge when Susan went home and repeated this conversation to her.

But Susan said, "No, we can't. I wouldn't sleep a wink all night thinking of the silkworms starving to death next door. Can't we just go and ask for some mulberry leaves ?"

"That's the one sure way not to get them," said Midge. "Macdonald the head gardener doesn't like children at all and hates us like poison—I can't think why, really, because we were awfully nice children, unless it was on account of Bill, who used to be bad about pulling up young seedlings to see how they were coming on—"

"Och well then," said Susan, "we'll just have to go in and pinch a few mulberry leaves."

"We ?" said Midge.

"Well of course—you'll have to show me where the trees are."

"You can't miss them," said Midge. "I'll point them out from our bedroom window. And I'll draw you a plan if you like."

"Och away," said Susan. "I wouldn't know a mulberry tree if I found one in my porridge. You must come and help me. I might go for the wrong tree."

"Well you might, I suppose," said Midge, "and there are some very rare trees there—rare for England, anyway—and Macdonald would probably kill you if he caught you monkeying about with those. There's a catalpa—oh, and a Judas-tree— that's *deadly* poison," she added helpfully.

Susan looked anxious. A savage Macdonald and a deadly poisonous Judas-tree! "There you are then," she said.

"Although now I come to think of it," said Midge,

"I think the Judas-tree is only poisonous to insects and birds—"

"You come with me," said Susan.

If the Gallery garden had been farther away than across the road, Midge would certainly have refused; however, she put her recorder down with a sigh and rose. "This is against my better judgment," she said, "but come on, then—"

The two girls went through the yard and round the house and Chang padded silently after them. "I don't know about Chang, though," said Midge doubtfully. "Macdonald doesn't like cats any better than he likes children."

"Well, it's not easy to make Chang change his mind when he thinks he's going for a walk," Susan reminded her. "Besides, surely nobody could object to my wee Chang ?"

Midge thought that Chang's charms might not be so obvious to Macdonald as they were to Chang's mistress, but she could not face the struggle of shutting a reluctant Chang up in the house. "Oh well," she said, "perhaps Macdonald has gone for his tea or something."

There was no sign of Macdonald in the garden. But on the other hand, there were no mulberry leaves either—not within reach that is. Great luscious thick branches waved above their heads— out of reach. Chang sharpened his claws on the trunk and climbed up the tree.

"If that cat was worth his salt he would throw some leaves down to us," said Midge. "As it is, we'd better go home."

"Och away," said Susan. "We'll have to climb the tree, that's all. Come on, give me a buckie-up."

"What, and have a great lump like you jumping on my back?" said Midge. "No thanks. You bend down and give me a buckie-up."

Susan said all right and bent down and clasped her ankles. Midge totteringly climbed on to her back and steadied herself against the tree-trunk.

"And whit might you two young leddies be doing?" said a disagreeable Scottish voice.

"Ow!" said Susan and collapsed, with Midge on top of her. They picked themselves up and gazed into the cold blue eyes of Macdonald.

"Well," said Susan. She could think of a lot of things they *might* be doing, but she didn't think it would be very polite to try to be funny. "Well," she said again, and then had a sudden inspiration, "it's my cat," she said. "He *is* so silly. Climbs up a tree and can't get down!"

There was a faint thump and Macdonald said, "He's got down this time right enough." The girls turned round and saw the faithless Chang, tail in the air, stalking majestically towards the gate "Good day to you," said Macdonald and stood inexorably waiting for them to go.

"Well—" said Susan and hesitated. "Well—good day," she said feebly and the two girls followed Chang.

"Old beast," said Midge. "He knows that we want something. Now he'll haunt this part of the garden until the gates are closed."

CHAPTER FOURTEEN

OPERATION SILKWORM

MACDONALD NEVER moved from that part of the garden for the rest of the evening, because Susan had a look at intervals from her bedroom window which overlooked Tollgate Road and the Gallery garden. There was a lovely view from there of the Gallery and the old chapel of Wichwood College and the garden—catalpa-tree, Judas-tree, mulberry-trees and all. Susan couldn't bear it—all those mulberry leaves and the poor unfortunate silkworms dying like flies next door. Even when she and Midge went to bed, worrying about them kept her awake for hours—well, for half an hour anyway, and when she did fall asleep she dreamt about Pea-green, which was a lot worse than insomnia in her opinion, so that when she next woke, and it was dark, she did not try to go to sleep again but switched on the bedside light and got up and dressed.

Then she proceeded to waken Midge. This was no easy task at the best of times; at one o'clock in the morning it looked like being hopeless. Susan eventually hit on the idea of shining her torch full in Midge's face and resolutely keeping the beam there in spite of Midge's wriggles.

Midge sat up at last. "What *is* the matter ?" she muttered furiously.

"Nothing's the matter," said Susan soothingly.

"I'm going to the Gallery garden to get mulberry leaves and I need you to come with me."

"Susie," said Midge, "you really have gone round the bend at last. Why can't you mind your own business?"

"Well, I can," said Susan, "but I can't lie here sleeping while poor dumb animals are dying next door."

Midge said crossly that she didn't see how silkworms could be classed as animals, dumb or otherwise, and what about all the other suffering dumb animals—lost dogs, starving cats, ill-treated horses, didn't they keep her awake?

Susan said, "They would if I thought about them, but I haven't any examples actually before my eyes, as it were, and the silkworms are *next door*!"

Midge wondered if it would be less trouble to hit Susan over the head once and for all, or to get up in the middle of the night and go capering off to the Gallery garden. She decided that after all life would be much much duller without old Susan bumbling about like a bluebottle against a pane of glass—and the Gallery garden was only across the road—and Macdonald's little cottage was right at the other side of the Gallery grounds— She rose and pulled on an old skirt and jumper. "Well," she said morosely, "here goes for Operation Silkworm." Susan beamed happily at her.

It was quite fun being out at that time of night. It wasn't a thing that often happened to Midge and Susan, and they felt bold and adventurous and strange. Nobody stirred as they crept downstairs and out of the front door, which they carefully latched lest it should bang shut with them on the wrong side of it. Outside it was still and silent, the great trees vividly green in the queer light of the street lamps.

"It's as bright as daylight!" Midge whispered, rather alarmed. "A policeman on his beat or anybody might see us—!"

"There doesn't seem to be anybody about," Susan whispered back, "and there are lots of trees on the other side—we can get over the wall in a patch of shadow. Come on—"

The wall wasn't high and they climbed it without difficulty. They dropped down silently on to the other side.

"Nothing to it," Susan whispered, when Midge clutched her arm.

"'Sh!" Midge breathed in Susan's ear. "There's somebody else in the garden! I got a glimpse just now out of the corner of my eye! Wait here and see if he moves again. I think he's under one of the mulberry trees—" Both girls stood tensed, straining their eyes. Suddenly Midge whispered again, "No, he isn't! He's over by the Gallery door! I could have sworn—"

"Maybe there's a gang!" quavered Susan.

"Don't be silly," whispered Midge. "What would a gang be doing here?"

"Stealing pictures," whispered Susan.

Midge gave a start of surprise. "*Susie*," she whispered, "perhaps you're right! He has something in his hand! And he's coming in this direction! What do we do?"

"C-c-catch him," said Susan in a valiant if rather shaky whisper.

"Yes, of course, but how ?"

"Och, just *grab* him—!"

"Be ready then—shall we rush out— ?"

"No, no, we might easily miss him—wait here in the shadows—he's coming towards us—!"

The stealthy figure left the shelter of the Gallery and darted from one patch of shadow to another until he reached the wall. He came slowly and cautiously in the direction of the girls. Suddenly Susan whispered urgently, "He's going over— *quick*—!"

They dashed out of cover and rushed to the spot where the figure was half-straddled across the wall. Each grabbed at a leg. The man thrashed out wildly and a boot crashed into Susan's face. She gasped with the sudden shock and pain but grimly held on.

"Pull . . . him . . . down," panted Midge. They pulled desperately; there was a sound of rending cloth; risking another crash on her face, Susan shifted her grip and held him securely round the ankle.

"I've . . . got . . . him," she grunted. "Pull him down!"

Both girls hung on grimly at the wildly flailing legs. At that moment the man's grasp on the top of the wall slipped and he crashed to the ground. Midge and Susan, taken by surprise, toppled over backwards.

"Quick! Quick!" gasped Susan, scrambling to her feet. "He'll get away!"

But the man lay still. "Golly," said Midge, "I think he must have hit his head on the path!"

"Dead ?" said Susan in a high-pitched squeak.

Midge, remembering that she was a doctor's daughter, thrust her hand under the man's coat "Heart's pumping away like anything," she said. "And there's this!" She drew out a roll of canvas and thrust it at Susan.

Susan moved into a patch of light and unrolled it. Both girls peered at the dark canvas, at the laughing, merry boys' faces that looked up at them. "Golly!" said Midge again, "I believe it *is* a Murilol from the Gallery—*Spanish Boys* it's called or something like that—it's frightfully famous!"

"Well!" said Susan exultantly. "We really have done something this time!"

Suddenly Midge came to her senses. "Tie him up quick before he recovers consciousness," she said. "And then we'll telephone Joe at the police-station."

"What do we tie him up with ?" said Susan. "I have a hankie but—"

"I have a hankie too," said Midge.

"Tie them together and then tie his hands behind his back," said Susan.

"Tie his feet surely," said Midge. "Then as he wakens up he won't be able to run away."

"If you tie his feet and he wakens up, all he has to do is bend down and untie his feet," said Susan. "Tie his hands—and tie his shoelaces together and that will cramp his style a bit—"

"Standing here arguing about how to tie him up," said Midge, giggling a little with reaction. "We'll lose him if we're not careful—" They busied themselves knotting the handkerchiefs together and securing the man's wrists behind his back. Suddenly a small sound made them look up. Cautiously approaching across the grass from the shadow of the mulberry tree came a small figure.

"Well for the love of Mike," said Susan, "it's our highly strung and temperamental Pea-green!"

"Hope he doesn't give a highly strung and temperamental yell," said Midge. "Hi, Pea-green," she called softly, "hurry up!"

The small figure advanced slightly more confidently.

"Have you got a belt ?" asked Susan.

"Naturally I have a belt," said Pea-green.

"Well, hand it over," said Susan.

"But I need it to keep my trousers up," said Peregrine.

"You can hold your trousers up," said Susan. "Hand it over. We need it to tie up this joker's legs."

Peregrine reluctantly unfastened his belt and handed it to Susan. "Bit of luck," she murmured.

"Who is he ?" asked Peregrine.

"Oh, just a burglar who was trying to steal an old master from the Gallery. We captured him," said Susan airily.

"Why didn't you come and help us, Pea-green ?" asked Midge.

"I didn't know you needed help," said Pea-green.

"We didn't," said Susan smugly.

"One of us had better go and telephone Joe now. Not 999—Joe must get the credit for this—" said Midge when the still unconscious burglar was safely secured. "And perhaps we'd better get Macdonald—"

"I'll telephone Joe," said Susan quickly.

"Pea-green," said Midge, "go round to Mr. Macdonald's cottage and tell him to come at once—"

"I don't know where it is," said Peregrine.

"Oh well, I'll go," said Midge. "Are you capable of staying here and guarding our prisoner ? Now that your hair's cut off you're not the Samson you were—"

Peregrine said coldly, "Of course I can guard the prisoner. I have a gun—" He pulled a gun out of his pocket, and Susan jumped and gave a little yelp.

"Relax, Susan," said Midge, who had a younger brother herself, "it's only a water pistol—"

Susan giggled shamefacedly and climbed the wall. Midge darted off in the opposite direction to seek out Macdonald. Peregrine, one hand holding up his trousers, stood astride the prostrate prisoner, his gun pointing down at him.

Of course it was too much to hope that neither of the grown-ups would waken; Susan had just made her telephone call to the Carmichaels' friend Joe the policeman at West Wichwood station when Aunt Lucy appeared in her dressing-gown. Susan gabbled an incoherent account of the affair at her and rushed upstairs to waken Bill and tell him what had happened. Before long the whole family was streaming across Tollgate Road in their dressing-gowns. Lights flashed on next door and Adrian came out. The police car arrived, and last of all came Midge with an irate and unbelieving Macdonald. As Susan said afterwards, it was the most exciting night of her life and even if Aunt Lucy gave them the most frightful row in the morning, it was well worth it.   In fact, she had only one regret—

"What's that?" said Midge, yawning and climbing into bed again after it was all over, even the cocoa and biscuits in the kitchen, "Och, I forgot the mulberry leaves," said Susan.

CHAPTER FIFTEEN

NICE MR. PILKINGTON

"WILL YOU ALL," said Aunt Lucy for about the twentieth time, "go and get ready for Mrs. Gascoigne's party?"

The family muttered rebelliously under their breaths, but eventually and reluctantly prepared to go upstairs to change. As she trailed across the hall, Midge caught sight of the evening paper sticking in the letter-box. She collected it and spread it out on the hall floor to read it, as she usually did. Suddenly she gave a yell of fury. The family gathered round and Susan rushed downstairs again. Midge was pointing a quivering finger at the *Evening Banner*. There, bang on the front page, was a photograph of Peregrine, handsome and smiling and holding his water pistol. Under it were large headlines:—

BOY (9) CAPTURES BURGLAR SINGLE-HANDED
OLD MASTER SAVED
DARING ROBBERY FOILED BY TOY PISTOL

and underneath *that* Susan and the Carmichaels, breathing heavily in their rage, read:—

Early this morning Wichwood Gallery was the

scene of a thrilling adventure for a small boy. Peregrine Gascoigne was worried about suitable food for his silkworms and slipped at night into the garden of the Wichwood Picture Gallery opposite his home in Wichwood Village to look for mulberry leaves. While there he surprised a man who was attempting to steal a famous old master, and single-handed held him up with his water pistol and tied him up with his belt and handkerchief and mounted guard over him until the police arrived . . .

Then followed a bit about how the man had presumably got into the Gallery and a bit about the picture and a bit about Wichwood Gallery being the oldest picture gallery in London and who had founded it and the famous pictures it contained which the Carmichaels didn't bother to read. And at the end came another piece which Midge read out through her teeth:—

Peregrine Gascoigne is the son of the well-known artist, Selina Gascoigne . . .

"Nothing about a well-known writer, Midge Carmichael, really doing all the capturing!" cried Susan when she could speak.

"*I* didn't," said Midge. "The whole thing was you, Susie. I'd never have gone near the place if you hadn't nagged on about mulberry leaves—!"

"And that little rat Pea-green," cried Susan, her indignation mounting as she recollected the night's doings, "didn't show face until we had the man tied up! All he did was lend his belt and stand over him with his footling water pistol!"

Charlotte marched off to the telephone. "I'm going to ring up the editor!" she cried.

"Well of course you can't," said Midge. "It would sound too feeble. ' Please sir, it wasn't Pea-green at all, it was my cousin and my sister—' What does it matter, anyway—after all *we* know that we caught the man—"

"Och- yes," said Susan, going slowly and mournfully upstairs to change for That Woman's party. "But *jings* it would have been great to have had our names in the paper!"

Aunt Lucy sent the young people on ahead to the party while she waited for Uncle Charles to come back from his last round of patients. Susan and the Carmichaels found the Gascoignes' front door invitingly open but nobody about. They rang tentatively, but no one appeared.

"Let's go in," said Bill.

"Let's go home," said Midge.

Gabrielle came lounging across the hall eating a pickled onion and saw them as they hovered uncertainly round the door. "Oh hallo," she said, "you're early," and having thus put them all at their ease, she went on: "Come into the garden. Selina's dressing."

"If you want to go and change," said Charlotte politely, "don't let us keep you."

Gabrielle, who was in her jeans and a moderately clean yellow blouse, said "I have changed," and glanced at the best clothes of the others, who immediately felt over-dressed. Gabrielle took them down the elegant little wrought-iron stairs that led from the drawing-room to the garden, her horse's tail bobbing as she went, and walked towards some garden seats. She suddenly noticed Susan's black eye. "What's the matter with your face ?" she asked indifferently.

"That's what Susan got from the burglar's boot," said Charlotte. "We saw that *Pea-green* got his photo in the *Evening Banner*."

"Oh yes," said Gabrielle, "wasn't it fun ? Adrian has a friend on the *Banner*. He was thrilled to get the story."

"*Not* a very accurate story," said Charlotte severely.

Gabrielle shrugged and said in a grown-up drawl, "Oh, you know what these reporters are—"

"They report what people tell them—" Bill began furiously, but Midge put her hand on his arm and shook her head at him. This wasn't a very promising beginning to the evening's party. She swallowed her rage and changed the subject. "Is it somebody's birthday ?" she asked. "That there's a party, I mean—"

"No," said Gabrielle. "Selina likes parties. And I expect she's going to announce her engagement to-night."

It was a wonder, Midge said afterwards, that Gabrielle didn't hear their hearts clanking down into their boots. They stared at Gabrielle, aghast. Oh why, oh *why*, thought Susan, didn't he tell us ? To let us hear it from this dreadful girl—!

Gabrielle looked at their astonished faces and

grinned. "Why should you be surprised at Selina getting married again ?" she said.

"We—we—we're not," stammered Charlotte. "I mean she's awfully young and pretty and not like a mother, really, at least—well, you know what I mean—!"

Susan's heart was bleeding for her cousins. Suddenly she couldn't stand it any longer. "Who to ?" she shot out.

"*My* school teaches us to say, *to whom*," Gabrielle said aggravatingly. "But haven't you guessed ? He was very old-world and gallant, he came charging in to see Selina after all the excitement last night and said that he wasn't waiting any longer, that she obviously needed a man to look after things—"

Susan thought, "I suppose they could always run away. I could help them—or they could come and stay with us when Mummy and Daddy come home from Africa—or would Aunt Lucy let them all live with her ? Perhaps Uncle Charles would come and see them sometimes— And poor little Bill—!" She bent her head and began to kick at a dandelion clump in the rather shaggy lawn.

"Well," said Charlotte and swallowed, "you couldn't have a nicer stepfather—"

"Oh ?" said Gabrielle. "I thought you didn't like him ?" Susan and the Carmichaels gaped at her. "I thought you always called him horrid Mr. Pilkington ?"

It wouldn't have surprised Susan if they had all dropped in a dead faint at Gabrielle's feet. She was the first to recover—slightly. She gave a nervous and high-pitched giggle. "Och away," she said,

" we didn't mean it. We think horrid Mr.—I mean, we think nice Mr. Pilkington is absolutely blissful and we think it's blissful that he's going to marry your mother and I hope you'll be terribly happy, if that's what you say to people who are having a step-father—and oh *jings*," she cried, turning to her cousins, "Isn't everything just as, as *blissful* as it can be, even if I didn't do it ?"

And beaming happily, she sat down in a deck-chair which, as it had been carefully arranged as a booby-trap by Peregrine, crashed to the ground underneath her.